GORDON

Pantheon Books, New York

GORDON

Edith Templeton

Author's Note: I wish to thank my agent, David McCormick,
for his ongoing support and devotion to my work.

All rights reserved under International and Pan-American Copyright
Conventions. Published in the United States by Pantheon Books, a
division of Random House, Inc., New York, and simultaneously in
Canada by Random House of Canada Limited, Toronto. Originally
published in Great Britain by The New English Library Ltd.,
London, in 1966.

Pantheon Books and colophon are registered trademarks of
Random House, Inc.

Library of Congress Cataloging-in-Publication Data

Templeton, Edith.
Gordon / Edith Templeton.
p. cm.
ISBN 0-375-42194-7
1. Scots—England—Fiction. 2. London (England)—Fiction.
3. Sadomasochism—Fiction. 4. Psychiatrists—Fiction.
5. Young women—Fiction. I. Title.

PR6070.E495 G67 2003   823'.914—dc21   2002070427

www.pantheonbooks.com

Printed in the United States of America
First Edition
2   4   6   8   9   7   5   3   1

Editor's Note

Gordon was first published in 1966 by The New English Library, under the author's pseudonym, Louise Walbrook. It was subsequently banned for indecency in England, as well as in Germany (where it was published by Stephenson Verlag), but not before selling well enough to attract the attention of The Olympia Press, the famous Paris imprint founded by Maurice Girodias in 1953 and the original publisher of such books as *Lolita, Story of O, The Ginger Man,* and *The Naked Lunch.* The Olympia Press retitled the novel *The Demon's Feast* and re-issued it in 1968 as part of its Traveller's Companion Series, the New York–based line of books whose dark green paperback jackets were familiar to "gentlemen" readers everywhere. The novel was also pirated and published in many languages, appearing around the world under various titles, and always under the name Louise Walbrook.

In 2001, Mrs. Templeton agreed to publish the novel, with its original title, under her own name.

Leben muss man und lieben; es endet Leben und Liebe.
Schnittet Ihr Par^en doch nur die beiden Fäden ^ugleich.
——GOETHE

One must live and love; life and love must end.
If only, oh Fates, you'd cut both these threads at once.

GORDON

Chapter

One

At a quarter to six in the afternoon on a sunny day in June, I was sitting near the bar counter at Shepherds watching a man above the rim of my glass. I was certain he was going to try to pick me up. I was less certain what I was going to do about it. In looks he reminded me of Major Carter who, a few weeks ago, had embraced me while taking me home in a staff car from a regimental dance and who, upon being repulsed, had apologised: "I can't think what came over me. And you such a nice girl, too."

Perhaps it was his disappointment at my being "such a nice girl" which had driven him to get drunk later on that night; or perhaps he had been drunk already in the car. I had lost sight of him as soon as we had entered the vast lounge of the hotel which was our mess. But half an hour later, while sitting and talking with several of my friends, I was astonished by Major Carter's appearance on the gallery which circled the lounge. He was naked except for underpants. Clutching the edge of the balustrade, he shouted: "I want a woman. I must have a woman!"

The two mess sergeants doing duty at the reception desk in the foyer, the mess secretary and a few other officers, among whom I saw young Dent, came running up the steps leading to the gallery and gathered round him. He was carried, struggling and shouting, to the lift.

What happened then was told me by Dent, who half an hour later joined the table where I was sitting. Dent was delighted:

3

"We get the fellow upstairs to his room and we put him on the bed and tie his hands and feet with two lanyards. Then we keep hanging about, talking, not really looking at him, thinking we'll give him another ten minutes and then his batman can settle him for the night and we'll call it a day, when he bursts his ties, ups and streaks out of the room and down the landing. We chase after him, he dashes to the door of the lift, opens it, and gets into the lift which isn't there. And we just close our eyes. A drop of four floors and down below a slab of concrete! We run down the stairs to pick up what's left of him, and when we get to the first floor, we catch sight of him running up the stairs to meet us, cursing and yelling, and we clash; and there we are all together again, fighting and struggling, just as before. He's in bed now."

On the following morning Major Carter, while eating his breakfast, was heard to remark that he was damned if he knew why he was covered all over with bruises.

I knew Shepherds well, from before the war, but I had never gone there on my own. Nor had I ever gone to any pub alone before.

It was 1946, the war was over, and I had returned to London two days before. I was twenty-eight years old, and though unsettled and lonely, I had not reached the phase in life of which it is said: "He who has no house now will not build one any more. He who is alone now will stay alone for long. He will awake, will read, will write lengthy letters, and will pace the avenues amidst the drifting leaves."

Shepherds had not changed, and I loved the very name of it— Shepherds in Shepherds Market, for the irony it carried, for being so exactly the opposite of what shepherds and a market implied. There was still the same ceiling, brown and glossy as though poured over with caramel, and looking so brittle as to make one convinced it would crack at the merest touch. The telephone at the right of the entrance was still enclosed in the antique sedan chair whose panels were painted with garlands of flowers, and there was still the one bartender who pretended that the half-crown he had received had been a florin.

The place was thronged, but I was out of the crush. I was seated on the low, wide windowsill near the second entrance, at the far end opposite the sedan chair, with plenty of space on either side of me to place my handbag and to put down my glass. I had on a short-sleeved slim-fitting dress of silk printed with wavering blobs of blue, pink, and mauve, recalling those marbled end-papers adorning the books of the nineteenth century. It was this dress I had worn one afternoon in the garden of our mess at Headquarters when Colonel Prior had exclaimed: "Don't move now, Louisa, whatever you do. You are looking just like a Renoir." It was this dress I had worn one evening when we were assembled in the ante-room and Major Turner had come in and said, "I've told the orderlies to wait dinner for another ten minutes. Louisa is looking so sweet just now that I didn't have the heart to break it up."

I was casting another glance at the man resembling Major Carter and observed that he had moved his stool yet another few inches nearer to where I was sitting. He was a blond, plump, red-faced young man; he would be, as we used to say, not overloaded with brains, and yet, at the same time, nobody's fool. Then I let my eyes stray farther down the room, gripped with disappointment at seeing only strangers. Shepherds was a meeting-place for anyone on leave from our crowd; and it was in the hope of finding, if not a friend, at least an acquaintance, that I had come here.

For a second I met the eyes of a man standing in front of the sedan chair, of which just one corner was visible and on it half of a painted rose, cracked and faded. Only his head and part of his shoulders were rising from behind a group of officers, sufficient for me to see that he was a civilian. Very smooth, I thought, something nasty there, too. Probably a Mayfair pansy. And I turned my eyes away and took a sip of my sherry.

While I watched from beneath lowered lids the progress towards me of the second Major Carter, I fell to wondering, as I had so often done before, about the deplorable logic of "and you such a nice girl, too." Surely, if a man despised a woman who had what is flatteringly called "granted him her favours," it must mean that he despised himself as well. The rare contrast to this was young Captain Dent with his "then, when I asked her to come to bed with me, she, being an intelligent woman, said yes."

The second Major Carter had just risen and taken a step towards me with a wondering, round-eyed stare and an open-mouthed smile, which made me certain that he would accost me with something like "What fun seeing you here. Now let me think— where did we meet before?" when I heard a very low voice saying, "We'll have another drink somewhere else." The voice was so faint and came so entirely out of nowhere that I thought for a moment I had been imagining it.

I turned my head.

The stranger whom I had dismissed as a Mayfair pansy was standing behind me. I was too taken aback to be able to speak. He detached my fingers from the glass I was holding and put it down on the sill. His hand closed round my wrist. I could feel the pressure of his hard thumb against my pulse. "Come along now," he said in the same low voice. I picked up my handbag with my free hand, and while the second Major Carter was still staring at me, round-eyed and open-mouthed but with the smile gone from his face, I followed the stranger through the door.

On the pavement he halted and released me. I turned towards him. We looked at each other. I was still dazed and bewildered over my inexplicable obedience. He was smiling.

Oh God, what have I let myself in for?, I thought as I looked into his eyes and found them decidedly unpleasant. They were deep-set, dark grey, and ringed with white, a peculiarity of the iris I had sometimes observed in very old people. But their almost sinister look derived probably from their placement. They were set at uneven levels, the left eye slightly higher than the right one. It must have been this which had given me my first impression of nastiness.

He was neither short nor tall, slender and narrow-boned, of an unimpressive physique I did not care for; and neither did I care for his face, though it held the same kind of fascination which informs the irregular and jutting outlines of a romantic ruin. The nose was high-bridged and uneven, the cheeks hollow beneath strong cheek-bones, the lips long, the chin beautifully and firmly rounded. The slightly waved jet-black hair grew low on to the wide forehead, underscoring the sombre pallor of the face like a cluster of dark ivy streaking down a flight of crumbling crenellations.

I glanced away from him, to the other side of the street where the watery sunshine of the late afternoon lay on the pavement. Then I looked at him again. He was not smiling any more. He was contemplating me intently.

"We'll go to my club in Brook Street," he said; "it's quieter there. Come along."

We crossed to the other side and walked a few steps, when I stopped in front of an antique dealer's shop-window. My companion stopped, too. I felt safe and reassured by the familiar sight of the bric-a-brac, the fans, the clocks, the beads, the snuffboxes, strewn on to a sheet of blue watered silk which cascaded down from the top of a Sheraton chest and was arranged in small ripples in the foreground.

"Do you care for that sort of things?" he asked.

"Yes," I said, "but they must be beautiful. I don't like things only because they are old. They must be beautiful as well."

He said as though talking to himself: "I see. Old and beautiful. Yes, I see."

I felt myself growing hot and was annoyed with myself for blushing, and wondered why he made me feel so embarrassed. I remained standing as I was, but ceased to pay attention to the antique litter and raised my eyes to the glass itself, on which our two figures were mirrored.

In his dark suit and white shirt he looked discreetly smooth and well groomed, in that confidence-inspiring and non-dandified style which Savile Row sheds on its devotees.

He was, I thought, in the professions, and a gentleman according to my own definition, by which I mean a man who has had Greek at school. And yet, despite the soundness of his attire, there was this face of his which clamoured to be portrayed by one of the masters of the Spanish or Neapolitan *tenebroso* painters, or to be modelled by the limelights of the stage. There was something of an actor about him, though not in the slighting sense of the term; I mean a first-rate man who would under-act and get his effect by throwing away his lines.

I said to myself, he's a barrister. Most barristers have a histrionic streak.

"I would not mind standing here for hours," he said, "if you were looking at the stuff. But you have been thinking about something completely different during the last minute or so. Trying to fit me in."

"Yes," I said.

8

"So we might just as well move on," he remarked; "this way. Come along."

"Sorry. It's quite true," I said. And as he continued to walk by my side in silence and never taking his eyes off me, I felt I had to say something.

"It's quite true," I repeated; "it's only that—actually, looking at ourselves in the glass—in the window of that shop—I always think there's something uncanny about mirrors and seeing one-self in them."

"Yes," he said, "why? Go on."

"For instance, Narcissus," I said, "who fell in love with him-self and pined away and died of grief because he could not reach himself and kiss his own image as he saw it in the water. The wa-ter was his mirror, of course."

"Yes," he said, "go on."

"Then there was the magic mirror," I said, "that made men fall in love with women, but only if they saw them in the glass and not in reality. Then there was the man who sold his reflection to a sorcerer and became friends with the man who sold his shadow to the devil."

"Go on," he said.

"Abraham Lincoln looked in the mirror one day and saw him-self looking over his own shoulder, and he knew what it meant— he was dead a few days later."

"Go on. What else?" he asked.

"There is nothing else," I said, "and you know these stories as well as I do."

"But you are pretty familiar with them," he remarked. "Why is that?"

He was right. My familiarity with these tales was unusual, and if I had not made it my business during the last year or so to col-lect tales about mirrors, they would not have come pouring out of me the way they had just done. But I had no intention of disclosing to him the reason for this preoccupation of mine, and I said therefore: "Well, yes. Naturally. I've known them ever since I can remember. I like them because they are strange."

"But how can they strike you as strange if you've always known them?" he asked. "The familiar is never strange. Only the unknown is strange."

I thought, My God, yes. Strange like you. And you are plenty. And I said with an uneasy laugh, "Yes, I suppose so. Really, you get me all tied up in knots." I was now sure he was a barrister—he had that way of taking you up on what you say till he made you look a fool.

He said, "Oh, no, I don't want to give you this impression. You may be tied up in knots, but not by me. I should say it is by your own fears. You should not have stopped yourself talking."

"But there was nothing else," I said.

"There was plenty else," he said. "Was, and is."

We were about to pass under the archway leading into Curzon Street when I pointed at the narrow door of the house adjoining the fruit store, saying, "Look, I stayed in this place once, for two months. Before the war. It was simply heaven. It belonged to a friend of my mother's, and she was ravishingly beautiful. But she's moved somewhere else now, and I haven't seen her since the beginning of the war, and I wonder what she looks like now. My grandmother was a great beauty, too, and she remained a beauty, even when she was old."

He said, "Ah, yes. The old and the beautiful. So we've come back to it again."

I told myself to speak to him as though he were Major Carter. I said, "Shepherds is all right for the first hour or so. But once it's after six it gets terribly crowded."

"Do you go there often?" he asked.

"No. I haven't been there for ages. I only went today because I've been away from London. Have a look round and get the feel of the place again."

"There are other ways of chasing one's memories, only one has to know how," he said. "Where have you been?"

"In Hamburg, with the army," I said, "and before that I was in Headquarters, in Westphalia, in the sticks. I only did a year, though."

"I was in Germany, too," he said, "and before that in North Africa, with the desert army," and, falling into the voice of an old man quavering with emotion, he added: "A just and noble war, fought with the help of our gallant allies," and he gave a grin of artificial cheerfulness, horribly inviting and frighteningly jolly, like a crocodile's smile.

"Yes," I said, laughing, and I fell to wondering again about that sinister, sardonic actor's quality of his. There was one part for which he was cut out—now I knew it; he was a "natural" for it, as Reggie Starr, the film director with whom I had lived for a year before going to Germany, would have said. He could have, to use Reggie's parlance, "walked on" without any make-up . . . It was, of course, the role of Mephisto in *Faust*, the role of the destructive, jeering intelligence. But there is nothing evil about Mephisto, and he is supremely good company, and I reproached myself for having imagined he was nasty only because he had queer eyes.

"Are you glad you are out?" I asked.

"Yes. I'm glad," he said; "but I'm not quite out yet. I'll be demobilised completely in five days' time."

"I'm glad, too," I said, "I could have stayed on. They asked me to. But I didn't want to. I'll never have such a good life again, though. But still."

"Then why did you leave?" he asked.

I gave the reply I had given to the brigadier when I had handed in my resignation: "Because it was a stagnation. A hot-house atmosphere. I want to be in London again, in the middle of things." It was the truth but only the edge of the truth. I had never told anyone the reason for my leaving.

"Here we are. This is the place," he said, stopping in front of a narrow-fronted shabby house. "It did not take long, did it?" And, falling into an unctuously declaiming voice, he added: "Time passes so pleasantly with good talk."

He went ahead of me, up two flights of mean stairs carpeted in green plush. We entered a long room. The bar near the door was brilliantly lit by sconce lamps, but the main part of the place was dim in the feeble light coming through the half-drawn curtains of worn cretonne at the far end. Against one wall stood an upright piano. A man and a woman who looked like husband and wife were serving behind the counter, with about four people on high stools facing them, and a man who must have been a guest—the club did not look as though it could afford an entertainer—was tinkling on the piano.

We went across to a settee placed against the window. It was covered with two flat cushions. As I sat down, my companion took the one from his seat and slid it behind my head. "You are looking very pale," he remarked.

"I'm always pale," I said.

"Yes, I realise that," he said; "your skin is very pale. But just now you are whiter than you should be. I think a whisky would be better for you than anything else."

I loathed whisky and yet I did not protest when he ordered the drinks. When they were brought, I took a sip, curled my lips with distaste, and said: "I don't like whisky. I never did. I had it for the first time when I was fifteen. A man give it to me behind my mother's back, at a reception at home. And I took it because it was so terribly daring. But now I don't care any more. It's all the same to me."

"You mean," he said, "that you don't have to pretend to be daring, because you actually are?"

"No," I said. "I've outgrown even that. I don't think it so wonderful to be actually and really daring. It's childish."

He said in the voice he had used before, as though talking to himself: "Outgrown. Childish. Your mother, your mother."

I looked at him, then turned away.

I was upset and flustered. He was observing me coldly, as though lying in wait, and his coldly fascinated air was all the more disconcerting as it held not a glimmer of admiration. It was obvious that I did not appeal to him as a woman. That this was true was still more obvious when I cast my mind back on what had happened up till now. Not only had he not paid me the slightest compliment, but he had also failed to take advantage of all those tiny opportunities of touching me which had presented themselves—such as placing a hand under my elbow when guiding me across the street.

I suppose he's just bored and wants someone to talk to, I said to myself; and just as well. Because I don't like him. And, still feeling his eyes on me, I added to myself: There's nothing to be afraid of. He can't do anything to me. And I recalled a saying of my grandmother's: "A woman can always defend herself. And when she doesn't, it's because she doesn't want to."

He said, "Outgrown. First it was the whisky and then it was something else, behind your mother's back. And now you think you've outgrown your mother. What makes you think so? Tell me."

"No," I said.

I was furious because he had guessed so much. "Why should I?" I added, and, seeing his sarcastic smile, I said, "I shan't because I won't and you can't make me, and there's nothing you can do about it."

He said, "All this saying of yours—I will and I will not and you can't and you won't—it is so futile."

My fury increased. "And I refuse to be impressed by you. It's just a trick of yours that you have, repeating one or two words of what I say, and sounding full of wisdom. And it doesn't add up to anything. It's just—"

"Go on," he said.

"It's just drivel," I said, glancing at him sideways. He was still smiling. More than that, he seemed to be delighted.

"Go on," he said; "whatever you say, it's nothing to what my patients tell me."

I said heatedly, "And a fat lot of good you'll be to your patients if that's all the wisdom you've got." Then I caught my breath. Patients, I thought. That means he's a doctor, not a barrister.

"Very likely," he said; "there is so little one can do. But it's amusing. You know, when I was working in an institution, there was an old girl, and every time I went to see her, she would say to me she was the mother of the prince. Then one day, on my visit, I said to her, 'But, mother, I am the prince, your son. Don't you recognise me?' She was furious. She wanted to hit me. But she couldn't. So she turned round instead and hit another patient next to her, quite a harmless old woman. Cracked her skull, too. One of the funniest things I've ever seen."

I looked at him, incredulous. "This is horrible," I said, thinking, patients again. But what kind of doctor is he?

"Fiddlesticks," he said; "and you quite enjoyed listening to it."

"I don't want to drink any more," I said. "I've had enough."

"Then you can watch me drinking."

"I don't want to," I said. "I want to go. I don't want to be with you. I know that's not a very nice thing to say, but I don't feel like being nice to you."

"You needn't be," he said with a deep smile. "It doesn't matter what you say."

While I had been speaking, I had been listening to my own words with amazement. I had never spoken like this to anyone else before; and for my rudeness I did not even have the excuse of being drunk.

I had already picked up my handbag, prepared to leave in the face of his indignation. Now as I saw his amusement, I felt helpless. I had not succeeded in insulting him after all. And because of this I determined to stay, telling myself that I owed it to my pride not to leave till I achieved something to upset him.

For a while we continued in silence.

Then he said, "Look over there. The two at the bar. Near the door."

The two men he pointed at were sitting with their backs to us. They were both middle-aged and portly. They were turned to each other, engaged in conversation, and during this one of them reached out with his hand, slowly and leisurely, took the wallet out of the other's coat pocket, held it behind his own back, took out the contents, stowed these away in his trouser pocket and then, unhurriedly, replaced the wallet where it had come from, while all the time looking into the other's face and keeping up the conversation.

"Oh, God," I exclaimed. "I've never seen anything like it."

"Haven't you?"

"You must go and tell him," I said. "It's shocking."

"Not at all," he said. "It's very funny."

I looked at him, aghast. He was clearly highly amused.

"We shall go now," he said.

"Oh, good," I said, rising quickly.

"Don't rejoice too soon," he said. "I shall not let you off yet. You find me very awkward, don't you?"

"Yes," I said.

I was glad to get down the green plush stairs and to find myself once more in the street, in the full clear daylight and the pale sunshine.

"I'm going to show you my garden now," he said. "I happen to live in a house with a very nice garden. I know you'll like it." And he added, assuming the unctuously declaiming voice: "Get some clean air after this pool of iniquity."

I laughed to cover my uneasiness. The garden of the house he lives in? First the garden and then the house and then his room and then his bed. But that's ridiculous, I thought. He's no Major Carter.

As though guessing my thoughts, he added, "It will have to be for a very short time only, though. I have to go out to dinner later on."

"That's quite all right," I said hastily. "I want to get home soon, too."

We walked towards Park Lane, and the last twinge of my doubtfulness vanished when we came to a halt by a bus stop. It occurred to me that if he didn't take a taxi, he couldn't be too keen on me—he was just out to kill time till his dinner.

In the bus he sat down beside me without touching me. We spent the ride in silence. I was looking out of the window and he was watching me.

We got out in South Kensington, and after a short walk we reached tall, grey cast-iron gates of which one wing stood ajar, and entered a garden which delighted me.

It was old and old-fashioned, decayed and dusty, with circular flower-beds set exactly in the middle of each piece of lawn, bordered by jagged whitewashed stones. The curving paths were scantily gravelled, the flowers tattered, the shrubs mangy, the high trees crowned with pitifully thin foliage; even the weeds sprouting on the edges of the paths looked tired.

The low sun was hidden behind a small cluster of clouds. The air was heavy and still. The sky had turned grey.

"It's lovely," I said. "It would be ghastly if it were bright and decently kept up. This sort of garden is only right when it is a nostalgic mess."

"I knew it would appeal to you," he said.

We entered one of the paths, walking slowly side by side. He was not looking at me, he was talking, and I did not listen. He seemed dull and ordinary and I was feeling dull and bored, too, and I could not understand how, less than half an hour ago, he had been able to rouse me to rudeness and anger.

For the next few paces I tried to pay attention to him. It was something about sitting on an officers' selection board, sometime during the war. He stopped, turning to me, and I, too, stopped, facing him. He does have queer eyes, I thought.

He was saying, "It was farcical. There just wasn't enough suitable officer material any more. The interviewing became—" He did not throw me and he did not push me. He took me round the waist and by the shoulders and bent me backwards. I was terrified I would fall, but when I touched a surface of cold stone underneath me, the surprise of encountering the stone relieved me of my fear. He laid me down; a hard edge cut into the backs of my knees while my feet were still on the ground, and as soon as I was fully extended, he was inside me. The whole was achieved in a matter of about four seconds. It was speedy and casual and effortless and at the same time seemingly impossible, like any virtuoso performance. And of course, nobody could have called it a rape; there was no struggle and no violence and no menace and no overcoming of a resistance. I was neither willing nor unwilling. I was nothing at all. I had not been given the choice to be either. I had not even been aware that there was a stone bench behind me when we had halted in our walk and he had broken off speaking in mid-sentence.

Prostrated as I was on the chill, hard surface, I felt utterly helpless. I had never before felt so helpless in my life. And he went on, as casually as he had started, neither embracing me nor holding me down. I closed my eyes. For all I knew he had his hands in his pockets. Then I hoped he would continue and was afraid he might stop, and almost immediately after this my hopes and fears were resolved and I felt like weeping with relief, but no tears came and I was shaken by dry sobs. I was still struggling for breath when he ceased.

He took me by the wrists and raised me into a sitting position. I kept my eyes closed. He slapped me lightly on the cheek and said, "You are my little girl," and then: "Come on, get up now."

I stood up and glanced at him. He was cold and grave, just as his voice had been cold and grave, without any kindness in it. The "You are my little girl" had not held any tenderness. It had been a matter-of-fact statement.

The same blunt grey light as before lay over the dusty garden; the sky was dirty white, but there was no sign yet that the sun was about to set.

I felt astonished, ashamed, and annoyed with myself for having, from this complete stranger, been given a pleasure with which I was familiar from what the French call *"les plaisirs solitaires"* but which no other man before had been able to give me in just this manner, I thought, and recalled my fury when he had said, over the whisky, "First it was the whisky and then it was something else."

The man who had given me, when I was fifteen, my first taste of whisky as a dare, behind my mother's back, was one of my mother's admirers. I did not know whether he was her lover at the time, but I was convinced he had been. I rarely saw him. He was not a steady friend of our house. He was only asked to the big dinners and at-homes. He was married, and his eldest son was two years younger than I was.

By the time I was twenty, and on duty in our drawing rooms during a gathering of about fifty guests, he took to assisting me in my tasks and even went so far as to follow me to the kitchen quarters where I had gone in search of a fresh supply of *petits fours*. It was there, with the hired chef and our sulky cook and two of our maids coming and going between and around us, that he invited me for a drive in the country on the following afternoon.

I had recently lost my virginity. I therefore felt that it did not matter, in any case, and though I was certain I would derive no pleasure from the outing, I accepted. I had always been jealous of my mother's lovers and the idea that I was taking one of them away from her and that he preferred me to my mother filled me with a deep satisfaction.

I did not care for him particularly. He was a good-looking, empty-faced, blank-eyed man of the world, devoid of passions and enthusiasms and given to trite conversation which was pleasing in so far as it demanded no effort to respond to it.

We drove to a small hotel standing in vast parklands, with no other buildings in sight. I had never before been to a hotel with a man, and I was impressed by his way, when we walked inside, of ordering tea to be brought upstairs, without even saying that he wanted a room.

As I undressed, he said to me, "Whatever you do, don't fall in love with me," and I felt contemptuous at his conceit.

He took me from the side, lying behind me; this surprised me as I had, up till then, believed that there was no other way of being taken except lying on my back. He slipped one arm under me and fondled my breast, and while penetrating me, he caressed me with his other hand between my thighs. I had never imagined it could be done. It was delicious.

When we were drinking tea, he said, "But you did very nicely. It must have been very good."

I did not reply. I was determined not to give him any grounds for self-congratulation.

I did not realise at the time what a rare and extraordinarily good lover he was, and that my attitude towards him was most ungracious. I also lacked the experience to appreciate the irony of the fact that this ordinary, harmless, modest womaniser possessed a skill of which the most spectacular conquerors are ignorant.

When he asked me when we could meet again, I said curtly that I did not know. I felt the main purpose had been achieved and that, though I would never tell her about it, I had at least in one point scored and got even with my mother. I never regretted my refusal to lie with him again, because my emotions had not been aroused. I had not thought about him for years.

Now on the stone bench it had been different. And the thought that this man whose name I did not even know had managed, without any additional effort on his part, to give me this pleasure by his short, indifferent, careless act, filled me with embarrassment.

"Come along now. I'll see you home," he said, taking me by the wrist.

This way he had of taking me by the wrist, as he had done when leading me out from Shepherds, made me resentful. It was an utterly one-sided gesture of taking hold of me, without bothering to demand and obtain my consent. It was like lifting a chair by its rail and dragging it over the floor to where one wanted to place it.

Why, at least, can't he take me by the hand, I asked myself as I walked by his side. But then, I'd never let him take my hand. I'd never fit my hand into his, and, filled with rebellion, I wriggled my arm and tried to evade his grasp. The fingers which up till then had been loose and cool over my pulse closed round me tightly.

"Don't withdraw from me," he said in a low, non-committal voice as though making a remark like "Mind this step."

"Leave me alone," I exclaimed.

"No, I won't leave you alone," he said, still in that same voice, as though warning me not to trip up.

He waited for a few seconds while I tried to wrench myself away, and then his other hand enclosed my elbow and his thumb moved slowly into the soft inner bend, feeling and exploring the flesh, the veins and the tendons, increasing the pressure and increasing the pain. It was not a sharp pain; it was blunt and enervating and sickening.

I cried out: "No, stop it. You are hurting me!" and his thumb dug deeper, and at the same time he twisted my wrist.

I had never before thought of my elbow as a place for peculiar sensations. Exposed to full view, it does not carry with it the erotic secrecy of the thighs and the breasts. And yet I felt now like belonging to him more shamefully and more deeply than I had done on the stone bench.

I went limp and put my head against his chest. The dark grey serge was faintly rough and hard and lifeless. I could barely sense him breathe, let alone hear the beating of his heart. He released my arm.

I was beyond indignation, beyond sulkiness, beyond truculence. I only felt the anger of disappointment. There I was, I had given in, I had admitted it by my movement of submission. And there he stood, without making the slightest gesture to acknowledge it or to reward me.

I straightened up, burning with humiliation. I thought, I should have gone for his neck and bitten through the blood vessels in his throat.

He was watching me. "Come along, say it," he remarked.

"Say what?" I asked.

"What you have just been thinking, what you'd like to do to me," he said.

"I don't want to do anything."

He gave me a sardonic smile. "You'll tell me next time."

"There won't be a next time," I said.

"Come along now, don't dawdle," he said; "you've been wanting to get out of here and away from me all along. Why are you stopping now?"

We went to the gates and he pulled one wing open for me, though this was not necessary, as it was still standing ajar. We went out.

"There won't be a next time," I repeated, in what I hoped was a haughty manner.

He said, falling into a shrill, yearning voice full of the agonies of the distressed lover, "Don't be so hard-hearted. Don't make me suffer so," and I had to laugh against my will.

We walked along the pavement in the deserted street.

"Then, you will see me again? Swear you will," he said, still acting the anxious lover. "Can't you see that I am willing to prostrate myself before you?"

"No, I won't," I said, smiling.

"Where do you live?" he asked.

"I won't tell you."

"Oh, dear, oh, dear, there you go again. I never had any luck with women. I wonder why?"

And I burst into laughter.

A cab came towards us and he stopped it. "Go to the West End," he told the driver. We got in. I settled myself in a corner and he was beside me, but not close.

It was still daylight in the streets, but the inside of the cab was filled with the intimate permanent gloom peculiar to carriages of its kind—an artificial gloaming exhaled by the aged, mummified leather.

I turned to him. In the flickering shadows the white rings circling his pupils stood out more sharply than before. He does have queer eyes, I thought, and he's queer altogether. My exhilaration had gone as soon as he had stopped playing the crushed lover, and he obviously had no intention of cajoling me, just as he had no intention of soothing me with a touch of his hand.

"Why did you pick me up?" I asked.

"Because I thought you were interesting," he said.

"Do you go to Sheperds often?" I asked.

"Yes."

"Do you like it?"

"Yes."

"Don't you find it gets frightfully crushy after six?"

"Yes," he said. "And stop it now. It's useless."

I turned away from him and looked out of the window.

"Oh, God," I exclaimed, "there's Derry and Toms already. And Pontings."

"Does it surprise you?" he asked.

"No, not really," I said.

"Then why do you pretend? I told you to stop playing for time," he remarked.

"Tell him to go up Church Street," I said, "and then turn

right. It's in Linden Gardens. But that doesn't mean I'm going to see you again. Even if you've got my address."

He said, "You remind me of a patient of mine, who told me he didn't like vaulting, but it wasn't that he was afraid to hurt his balls. When somebody says it isn't that, and it doesn't mean that, he only tries to deny the truth. Because it always *is* and it always *means*. Will you stop pretending now?"

Chapter

Two

He had told me to meet him at Shepherds two days later, at six in the afternoon.

I put on a red cotton dress with white dots and white zig-zag braiding outlining the seams. It was akin to a kitchen-maid's frock. I looked in it a "slip of a girl," and as near as I could get to looking like a floozie. It was made from the same pattern as my elegant, well-bred silk dress of the other day, but because of the humble material it had this entirely different character. I had yet a third dress made of that same pattern. It was of thin dark blue wool, with long sleeves; I had worn it for my interview in the War Office when applying for a job, and I imagined that it made me look serious, studious, and reliable.

On this afternoon I had chosen the red cotton on purpose. I hoped it would imply how little I wished to please him. I believed I did not care whether I pleased him or not. Yet I fiercely resented how he had treated me in the garden that night, and I hoped to hurt him by showing my indifference. It need hardly be said that I arrived, purposely, a quarter of an hour after the appointed time.

He was standing at the same spot where I had had my first glimpse of him, with his back against the flower-strewn panel of the sedan chair.

He was in uniform, in battle dress and beret, with the insignia of a major. It did not suit him. The coarse material of the baggy tunic made him appear shorter and slighter then he was; the beret hid the devilishly attractive hairline; the khaki turned his pallor to sallowness.

"I'm afraid I'm late," I said, determined to point out my insulting tardiness, in case he might not have noticed it.

He said, "You mean you are late because you are afraid."

For an instant I looked at him. Then I cast my eyes to the ground.

"I've put on my uniform for the last time today," he remarked, "as a swan song." His voice became wheezing, quaking, trembling with the emotions of a very old man: "As a heartfelt tribute to all the dear brave boys who gave their lives and their all to the cause of the fatherland," and then, as I was giggling, he resumed in his ordinary tone, "Let's get out of here."

Again he took me by the wrist; this time I did not resent it. Outside, he halted, raised my hand and held it away from him at a distance, shifting it slightly, so that the light struck a sparkle from my wedding ring.

He said, "This thin band of gold does not seem to weigh heavily on that little hand of yours."

"No," I said.

He lowered my hand and fell in step beside me, still holding my wrist.

"When did you walk out on your husband?" he asked.

"How do you know I walked out on him?"

"You are very good at walking out on people altogether, I should imagine," he said.

"I don't know," I said, "I've never thought about it."

"It was merely an idle observation of mine," he remarked. "You needn't think about it. When did you walk out on him?"

"Three years ago." I was certain he was going to question me about the reasons for my having left my husband, and I was determined not to tell him. I was therefore astonished when his next question was of an entirely different nature.

"How old was he then?" he asked.

"Twenty-seven," I said.

"So he was not old and beautiful, was he?" he remarked with a satisfied smile.

"Don't be so idiotic," I said. "What's that got to do with it?"

"How should I know?" he said, still smiling. "You should know. But as you don't seem to like the idea, don't give it another thought."

"You are really quite idiotic," I said. "It's like the man who was given the secret of how to make gold out of stone, with all the right rules and regulations; but while he was to do it, he must not for a second ever think of white elephants. And of course he couldn't stop himself thinking of white elephants. So why do you tell me, don't think about it? Because now I will."

"Of course you will," he said; "but it won't get you anywhere."

"Where should it get me? I don't understand you," I said.

"You don't have to understand me, my poor child," he said.

"You are talking nothing but rot," I said haughtily. I was elated because I was able to be as rude to him as I liked. I had never enjoyed such freedom before. I was drunk with my own impertinence. "Just because you say something nonsensical you imagine it's going to sound clever. It's like the poetry of T. S. Eliot. Nobody understands him and everybody says it's clever. And don't call me 'my poor child.' I hate it."

We had been walking along Piccadilly, and now he came to a halt in front of an antique shop. "Here," he said, "this will soothe you. And now, tell me why I shouldn't call you 'my poor child.' "

"Because it's so sad," I said, "There is a poem by Goethe— 'Mignon's Song.' And it's in it. *Und alle Bilder stehn und sehn Dich an, was hat man Dir, Du armes Kind getan?* I always feel like weeping when I read it. Of course you wouldn't know it."

"I did know it," he said. "Tell me the whole, roughly. How does it go?"

"She wants him to go with her to Italy," I said.

"Who is he?" he asked.

"Her father," I said, and added hastily, "No, sorry. I've messed it up. It's not quite clear who he is. Because in the first verse she calls him her lover. That's with the oranges and lemons. In the second verse she calls him her father. That's where the bit with the statues and the pictures comes in, and that sadness with the 'my poor child, what have they done to you?' . . . It's heartbreaking. That's why I don't like it," and I turned from the shop-window and raised my eyes to him.

"Go on," he said. There was again on his countenance that cold, fascinated attention, the look of lying in wait.

I grew flustered. "Then it gets wild and gruesome. High crags and dragons and rushing floods. You have to go over them and through them, if you want to get to Italy."

"And what does she call him in this verse?" he asked.

"She calls him 'my protector,' " I said. I added, "You don't know much, do you?" and gave him an arrogant look.

He did not seem to notice it. "It's excellent," he remarked; "it's most interesting."

"Of course it's excellent," I said; "it's Goethe. Goethe always is."

"I was not thinking of Goethe, my poor child," he said. "I was thinking of you. You have a lovely brain."

I was astonished by his compliment, though not pleased. It

was not the kind of praise I wanted. Besides, it was not true. Anyone could have given a crude rehash of "Mignon's Song."

"You are very easy to please," I said as we continued on our way. Yet, somehow, his "You have a lovely brain" had appeased me and I had stopped resenting his calling me "my poor child."

We had drinks in a pub in Shaftesbury Avenue. He took a double whisky and I had a sweet sherry which, to my relief, he ordered without comment.

"I'll take you to a Chinese restaurant now," he said.

"Oh, I know an awfully good one," I cried.

"That's not the one I mean," he said.

"How do you know the one I mean is not the one you mean?" I asked.

"Because you mean another one," he said.

"Well, what's yours called?" I asked.

"Bellevue," he said.

"You are cretinous," I said; "that's not Chinese."

"Oh, but definitely," he said, "Bellevue is Chinese for chopsticks."

He took me to a place in Wardour Street, and I was glad it was not the one in Shaftesbury Avenue which had been in my mind. It would, I felt, have spoilt my dinner if we had gone there; and it would not have been a case of "chasing one's memories," as he had expressed it the other day, it would have been a case of my memories chasing me. Never mind, I said to myself; it would all come right, now that I was back in London. And in the meantime, what did I care? He ordered the dishes without asking for my approval, but I did not resent it. On the contrary, it pleased me, though I would have taken exception to it with anyone else.

He just isn't my type, I told myself, that's why I don't care. And he is looking his worst today, in uniform.

At one point, while he was talking, there was a drop of gravy trickling down his chin; I gloated over it and did not tell him about it; I was quite disappointed when he wiped it off with his napkin a second later. I would have dearly liked to see him ridiculed and humiliated. I knew he would be taking me to where he lived as a matter of course and that I would go with him. But I had the idea that it did not matter as long as I did not care for him, and that if I managed to convey to him that he was unattractive to me, I would have achieved my aim.

After dinner we took a bus from Regent Street. It was not a number going to South Kensington or anywhere near it. I supposed he was taking me to another club. We got out in Portman Square, crossed over and halted in front of a tall old house, very well kept up and with an impressive black-painted door. He let himself in with his own key.

"This way," he said, and unlocked a door a few steps down the entrance hall. "Just this for the time being. I moved into here yesterday. I must now seriously look round for a place in Harley Street. Come in."

We entered a little hall and he led me into a fair-sized room. It was furnished in blond wood, in a bastard style of bow legs and crests of carved posies and knotted ribbon, faintly suggestive of Louis Quinze, with a moss-green fitted carpet and cream-washed walls. There was a quilted, buttoned settee covered in dark green wool to match the seats of the chairs. A desk stood near the window. The divan bed was made up, with the green brocade cover folded over the foot end and, without glancing at them, I knew that the curtains would be of the same brocade.

It was a decent, sub-luxurious room in an expensive neighbourhood, conforming exactly to its type, down to the colour scheme of blond cream and green, complete with the copper ashtrays, the pressed-glass vases imitating crystal, and the print of a sailing ship on stiff white-capped late-eighteenth-century waves. I knew that the bathroom off the hall would have tiles without a single crack in them, the wash-hand basin would be spacious and oval, the bath would be encased in panels of black glass, and the floor would be of black white-veined marble.

At a glance, I saw that there was nothing in the room belonging to him, and I was glad of it. I have always had a poor opinion of people who tell me they can transform the despair of a rented furnished bed-sitting room into a place of homely cosiness with a jug filled with flowers, an embroidered cloth, and a few pictures.

I was just then living in a room, too, much smaller, shabbier and poorer than the one we were in, in the attic of a boarding-house, with the bathroom and the lavatory three flights below on the ground floor, and I had not tried to "transform" it with those touches of "personal magic." I am an extremist. If I cannot have everything, I want nothing. Besides, at that time, I was content. I did not have the yearning for a home of my own which is supposed to claw at every woman's heart.

"I've got nothing to drink," he said.

"That's all right," I said, "I wouldn't want a drink, anyway."

He began to pace the room. "When you go to the bathroom," he said, "be careful. The basin might come crashing down on you. I'll have a new one put in tomorrow."

"I will be careful," I said, sitting down on the settee.

"I had a girl here last night," he said, "and I threw her out. She went into the bathroom, knocked a jar from the shelf and cracked the basin."

"How do you mean?" I asked. "You threw her out because of it?"

"Yes," he said, moving about, opening drawers in the chest and shutting them.

"But why?" I asked. "You really threw her out because of it? She didn't do it on purpose."

"I know," he said. "But it was done on purpose just the same. It was an act of spite against me. I can't be bothered with that sort of thing. Not from her, anyway. I couldn't be bothered with her altogether."

I remained silent. I asked myself if I was glad that a rival had been removed. I was not. I did not care either way.

"Get undressed and go to bed," he said without turning round, still busy with the chest of drawers.

I went over to a chair near the divan and slipped out of my dress, and while I did so, he left the room. Perhaps he did it on purpose, to spare any feelings of modesty I might have had; but I rather thought not. I took off my underwear and lay down on the bed. I turned on my side with my face to the wall and with my legs crossed and curled up, determined not to be agreeable in any way.

I had never behaved like this with a man before. I believed that once one went as far as to consent one should go through with it as nicely as one could, whether one enjoyed it or not, and that it would have been bad manners to do otherwise.

But with him everything had been out of the usual, starting from the first moment at Shepherds, and as he was the only man who ever had taken me without my consent, I felt free to behave as badly as I wanted to. I was rude to him in my talk; why should I not carry it through in bed as well?

He came over to me, and I bent my arms over my face and clenched my crossed legs still more tightly. I expected he would lift my arms from my face and kiss me, and melt my resistance in this manner, and I was determined to avoid it.

But he slid his hands round my hips and under them, and

raised them and turned me over, so that in a flash I was on my back, and with his hard bony knees he pressed into the soft inner part of my thighs, and as I gave way under the pain, he forced them apart and took possession of me in the easy, casual way he had done before.

But this lasted only for a few moments. Then he drove himself more deeply through me, and still more, and still more deeply, reaching depths which I had not known were inside me to be touched. It hurt and it was overwhelmingly outrageous, and I moved and tossed about, and tightened my inside muscles against him, to prevent myself from being invaded, but he seemed to be quite unaware of my distress and went on with a slow, steady, relentless determination, fastening me to him more tightly with each move.

I knew I could not fight him and I knew I could not get away and that I had to accept him. My arms fell from my face and I glanced at him for a short while. He was gazing into space. He did not see me looking at him. His sombre face was quite far away and above me, his brows were drawn together, and there was a bitter crease tightening either side of his mouth. I closed my eyes, and while I suffered the ever-returning knocks of pain inside me, I put my arms down by my sides, with my palms upwards, and wished he would, at least, place his hands in mine. He did not.

When he came down on top of me with the full length and weight of his body, but still not clasping or embracing me, I thought this would bring him to the end at last. I was mistaken. But he moved inside me differently now, without hurting me, more carefully, as though probing. As I relaxed with relief, he suddenly stabbed me with such sharp insistence that I cried out. It was really a repetition of the scene in the garden near the gate, when I had wanted to free my wrist and he had forced me to submit, and then, when I had surrendered, had refused to reward me.

And with unflagging thoroughness he went on. I became nearly senseless. Sometimes I heard myself gasping or screaming, but as I had ceased to have thoughts and almost ceased to have emotions, I did not realise any more why I gasped or why I screamed. And he went on. There is a saying, "No hour strikes for him who is happy," and this was true in my case as well, though I was beyond happiness or sadness. I could not imagine that he would come to an end. I was not even aware of myself any more; there was just enough left of me to be aware of him, only of him, and all the time. And he went on.

I did not realise at what point he reached the climax of possessing me. His breathing remained as soundless as it had been, but there was a change in the pressure of his body and then a stillness; I was too exhausted to understand what it meant. I did not know when he left me. I felt light and floating in the stillness as though the bed-sheet were a sheet of silent water, till I felt his fingers underneath my head at the nape of my neck.

I opened my eyes and saw him sitting on the edge of the bed clad in a dressing gown. I closed my eyes again and turned my face away from him and felt that he was pulling the pins out of my plaits and heard the clatter as he placed them on the bedside table.

I was wearing my hair, which was well over waist-length, like a tiara formed of two plaits. It was the traditional Gretchen style, so called after the heroine in Goethe's *Faust*, a coiffure never encountered in the circles I moved in, and commonly associated with the country girls of the Alpine regions.

Apart from its being unfashionable, it did not suit me. I was not a Gretchen. I was not fair and clear-eyed, I had no round pink face and no snub nose. I was neither demure nor naïve nor shy. And yet, I did have the one essential Gretchen quality, only I did not know it then; it was still hidden, but he must have discerned it at once.

Gretchen is seduced by Faust with Mephisto's help, has a child, goes mad, drowns the child, kills her mother, is responsible for her brother's death, is cast into prison, and is executed. I do not mean to say that anything of this was in store for me. I only mean that he must have guessed in me the same willingness to go under, to play Gretchen to a Mephisto-driven Faust.

The clatter ceased. He said: "All these dreadful weapons, these pins and daggers, you carry in your hair. You put them in on purpose, to injure me. You'd love to injure me, wouldn't you?"

I did not reply.

He tugged at one of my plaits and loosened it and laid the unwound strands over my shoulder.

"And yet, I am so kind to you," he said. "Here I am, even undoing your hair. So very kind. Just like a kind father."

I sat up and said heatedly, "Yes, you are quite right. I'd love to injure you."

He looked at me with a delighted smile. "You react so beautifully, it's a joy," he said; "just one simple, common, ordinary word, and you are up in arms."

"Which word? How do you mean?" I asked.

"I'll tell you another time," he said. "I don't want to have you upset. I must humour you now, you are still weak. Come, lie down again, and we'll have a nice, quiet talk. Only nice, pleasant things."

I lay down again.

He started to unwind and spread out my second plait.

"Why do you wear your hair so long?" he asked.

"I've always wanted it long," I said, "but my mother—oh, who cares."

"But your mother what?"

"She never let me have long hair. I always had to have it cut short and tied to one side with a satin bow. So terribly childish."

"But you were a child at the time, weren't you?" he said. "So, why should you have minded so much that it was childish?"

He said it in a soothing, consoling tone of voice, as though merely in order to keep the conversation going, for the purpose of "I must humour you now," and I, lying with my eyes closed, said wearily, "Yes, of course, I was a child. You are amazingly stupid with your remarks," and I started to laugh.

"What made you laugh now?" he asked.

"I thought of something," I said, "a line of a poem by Kaestner. In German. You wouldn't understand."

"I do understand some German," he said, "tell me."

I said, "It's, *ich wurde einst als Kind geboren und lebte dennoch weiter.* And in case you don't get it, it means, once upon a time I was born a child. And despite this, I went on living."

"It's very clever," he said, "but you are side-tracking me. Why didn't your mother let you have long hair?"

"I thought you'd forgotten by now," I said.

"Oh, no," he said, "and why did you want to have long hair?"

"I wanted to have it because she had it, too, when she was small. So why couldn't I, if she could? It wasn't fair. And there was one day of the year when my mother was allowed to wear her hair long and open down her back. That was on the emperor's birthday. She had it all. And when I was born, in 1918, the old Emperor Franz-Josef was dead and there was the break-up of the empire and we lived in a republic with a president, and of course, he wouldn't dare to have a birthday. She had had everything and I had nothing. Neither the emperor nor the long hair."

"But that's all so long ago," he said. "Why do you still think it is so nice to have long hair?"

"Because of the Empress Elisabeth," I said, "the empress of Austria. She wore her hair in a crown of plaits, much higher than mine, and she was the most beautiful woman of her day. Even the Empress Eugénie was a rag compared to her."

He said, "And you think of yourself as the Empress Elisabeth. And you'd like to open your hair for the emperor. No man sees a woman with her hair open except when he goes to bed with her. You didn't want to open your hair for me. I had to do it myself. You want to keep it for the emperor."

I opened my eyes. He seemed amused. I turned my face to the wall.

"Don't be so idiotic," I said, "it's a beastly habit you've got. First one tells you something perfectly decent and ordinary and you twist it till it sounds indecent and extraordinary."

"Just what I thought," he said. "I knew straightaway we'd get a lot of pleasure out of your long hair. We'll go on about this long hair."

"For how long?" I asked. "For the next half hour?"

"Oh, no," he said, "for longer."

"For two hours?" I asked.

"Oh, no," he said. "Longer."

I turned round and sat up. "For how long, then?"

"At least six weeks," he remarked, "I should say."

"For six weeks?" I asked, "talk about nothing but my long hair?"

"Yes," he said.

"You are pulling my leg!" I exclaimed.

"I am quite serious, my poor child, I assure you," he said.

"And it won't bore you?" I asked.

"No," he said.

"But what is there to talk about?"

"You'd be surprised," he said; "but you'll go to sleep now. Come on, get up, and go to the bathroom first."

I felt myself go hot and blush. I was greatly embarrassed. I remained as I was, sitting on my heels, with the top sheet clutched to my throat.

He was looking at me gravely and intently. "And I don't mean you should go and wash," he said. "Tell me how you say it."

"Spend a penny," I said.

"No, spend a penny is not right," he said, "because that's English, and English isn't your mother-tongue. How did you say it in your nursery days?"

"Loo-loo," I said, laughing to cover my embarrassment.

"That's better," he said. "Go and loo-loo."

"That's not the right way to say it," I remarked, feeling delightfully superior. "You don't loo-loo. You make it." And then, as he was still watching me seriously and intently, I fell back into my embarrassment. "Anyway," I said, "I don't want to. I don't feel like it. Leave me alone."

"I'm going to have so much trouble with you," he said. "Come on, now. You haven't been for hours. You are like a little girl of five; one has to think of everything for you."

My uneasiness and shame left me and I was flooded by relief and gratitude, as though I had been liberated from a burden which had been weighing on me for a long time. No man ever— for that matter, nobody ever—since my childhood days had told me to go and make loo-loo, or whatever one might call it. It was an absurd situation which should have made me indignant; yet, I liked it.

I put my legs over the edge of the bed and hesitated. I looked at him to see if he was not jeering at me, after all. He was not. He was still watching me intently.

"Stand up slowly," he said; "you are still weak. Shall I come with you?"

"Don't be so ridiculous," I said, laughing.

"Oh, dear, oh, dear," he said, "I'm always so unlucky with women."

I took a few steps across the room, when he said, "Steady. You are not the Empress Elisabeth, you are not at your coronation now," and he went up to me and detached my clasped hands from my breast, against which I was still clutching the sheet, took the sheet and flung it on the bed.

"You are a bit dazed, aren't you?" he said.

"Yes," I said.

I went to the bathroom, and when I had finished, I wiped myself with the paper and found that I was sore and swollen between my thighs; the edges of my lips were bruised, as they had been after I was deflowered.

I'll never tell him, I thought. I shan't give him that pleasure. And I don't even know his name. I'll never see him again. He is a beast.

But with my indignation there flowed a satisfaction, like the mingling of wine with water, that he had not only held me in his power and inflicted pain on me but had left the painful traces of his possessing me on my body. I wish I could have been deflowered by him, I thought, instead of that fool ox of a man at that time, and, taking one more piece of paper, I wiped myself once more and looked to see if there was any blood on it. My virginity had been lost in a small pool of blood. There was not a trace of blood on the paper now, and I regretted it.

I returned to the room and got into bed. I heard him move about and imagined he was putting on his pyjamas. When he got into bed with me, he was naked.

I made room for him, squeezing myself tightly against the wall, and he lay down in the middle, on his back and with his eyes closed.

The lamps were still burning, one on the bedside table and one on the desk. I did not dare to tell him to put them out. I lay down on my side, rested my head on one outstretched arm and bent the other arm over my breast, as I always did when I settled down to sleep.

I heard his voice: "Don't withdraw from me."

I turned round. And though he was still the same as before, on his back and with his eyes shut, and though his voice had been calm and even, a shudder seized me. It was no use denying any more what I had not wanted to admit from the first moment at Shepherds, and what I had paraphrased to myself by thinking, He does have queer eyes. I was afraid of him.

I rolled over hastily and began a hurried search for comfort against his body, like a dog turning round and round on a cushion before curling himself up for rest.

His body was pale, skinny and bony. His shoulders were no wider than his hips; he had what is called a six o'clock figure, straight up and straight down, a skimped and scanty physique, as though the fairy of miserliness had presided over his conception. It was not only unlovely to look at; it was uncomfortable to lie with, and I thought with longing of the large, fair, heavy body of Reggie Starr, with whom it had been so pleasant to cuddle up for the night.

I lay down close to him, hoping he would take me into his arms. He did not move.

I got on to my side and tried to curve my body round his. He remained extended as he was and I had to abandon the attempt. I turned with my back against him, hoping he would find it agreeable to make a niche with his body for me to nestle in. He stayed as he was.

Then I flung myself half across him and placed my head in the hard hollow between his throat and his collar-bone. He did not move. Only his lowered lids closed more tightly over his eyes. I was shaken by trembling. I had never known before what it was to tremble; I had only heard about it and read about it.

I lay there and could not stop trembling.

He said, "My sweet child." My trembling ceased. He still had not kissed me or embraced me or fondled me. I fell asleep straightaway.

When we were in our teens, my cousin Sylvia and I, we used to go to the mountains during the Christmas and Easter holidays, and we always told each other that when we were in the mountains we slept differently from the way we slept at home. At home we slept what we called "slow," and in the mountains we slept "fast." We meant by this that at home, upon waking, we had the feeling that we had been asleep for the good long necessary hours required for rest; whereas in the mountains we slept just as many hours, and yet, upon waking, though feeling bright and refreshed, we had the conviction that we had been asleep for fifteen minutes only.

This first night I slept with him, I was sleeping "fast," too, and this illusion persisted during all the many nights I shared his bed, resting on his uncomfortable body.

In the morning, when I opened my eyes, I found him sitting on the edge of the bed, fully dressed and smoothly groomed.

"Get up and get ready," he said. "I'll take you home now."

I got dressed and then I went into the hall, stood in front of the tall mirror and arranged my hair hurriedly and untidily with my small pocket comb, which was inadequate. My make-up was worn off, I had nothing with me to freshen it up, and though I had a lipstick in my handbag, I disdained to use it, convinced that the rouge on my lips would only underscore my bedraggled state.

I returned to the room. He was leafing through some papers on his desk. I was glad he did not look at me and I sat down on the settee.

After a while he said, without glancing up, "Are you ready?"

"Yes," I said.

"Why didn't you say so?" he asked.

"I didn't want to disturb you," I said.

"I see," he said, "and if I'd been sitting here for another hour, would you still not have said anything?"

"Of course I wouldn't," I said.

"I see," he remarked, rising from his chair and giving me a long look. "We'll go now."

I cast my eyes down. I felt furious. I had admitted that he was my superior and that I considered myself to be the underling.

It was only when he said "Come, my poor child" that my resentment fell away from me and I was at peace.

Before we left, he gave me his card and I put it in my handbag without glancing at it.

On the way he did not speak and neither did I.

When he left me at my door, he said, "You'll come to my place today at three," and walked away without waiting for my answer and without bidding me good-bye.

I looked at my watch when I got to my room. It was only half past eight. I would have slept till ten if I had been on my own.

To hell with him, I said to myself. I would have a bath first, I was dying for a bath, and breakfast after, but instead of getting out of my clothes at once, I went over to the glass and looked at myself carefully and for a long time, worried over my slipshod appearance and debating with myself whether it had disgusted him or not. To hell with him, I repeated, and added: As though it mattered. What do I care?

The day was Saturday, and I imagined that it was because of this that he was free so early in the afternoon. He might have taken it for granted, for the same reason, that I would be free, too. I might have been employed. He knew nothing about my circumstances. But even if I would not have been working on a Saturday afternoon, it still did not mean I would be disengaged. I could have had a rendezvous with another man, for all he knew. And yet he had never doubted that I would come to Portman Square.

The cheek, I said to myself while running my bath, who does he think he is? And then, remembering his card, I ran up the three flights of stairs, grabbed my handbag so as not to waste any time by fumbling, and skipped down the stairs, colliding with Mr. Sewell.

"What's the matter now?" he said, seeing me in my bathrobe and clutching my handbag. "That's a nice get-up for going out and meeting the boyfriend."

"My bath will be running over," I said.

"And a jolly good thing if it does," he remarked. "I could just do with a bit of accidental flooding. I might squeeze a new bath out of the insurance. What do you expect, you people? You expect the Ritz for the rents you pay. Knock at my door if you want me to scrub your back, will you?" And he disappeared into that part of the passage which led to the basement stairs.

I liked Mr. Sewell. He was a lower-class version of the stepfather of one of my class-mates, from whom I had received my first kiss. He was lean, smart, and breezy like him, an ex-officer like him, and, like him, he was a kept man. My class-mate's mother, who was a dressmaker with a large establishment, had kept this husband of hers for the sake of his charm; as far as I knew, he had never done any work at all. Similarly, it was Mrs. Sewell who wore the money-pants and the business-pants. She owned the rooming-house. She owned several other houses besides, looked after them herself, and gave him something to do by making him act as our landlord, which he did by making fitful appearances, mostly in the mornings, and slapping the Irish maid's bottom to "make her work better," to which she responded with cries of feigned indignation.

As soon as I had locked myself in, I got out the card. I read, "Dr. Richard Weir Gordon."

I might just as well see him this afternoon, I said to myself, as long as I get off in time for dinner tonight. I had been invited for a meal by my cousin Sylvia and her husband.

I did not think any further about it till, at two in the afternoon, I found myself in the hall ringing up my cousin Sylvia and telling her I would not be able to come to dinner that night.

When I got to the black front door in Portman Square, I found that it stood slightly ajar and I entered slowly, taking in at leisure the black-and-white-lozenged marble floor of the spacious hallway and the two Japanese vases, monstrously tall, which flanked the gilt console table, on which several letters were laid out. I stepped nearer and glanced at them, thinking that some of them might be for Gordon and, if so, could furnish me with a clue about him. Then I rang his bell.

When he opened the door and I entered, he said: "By the way, did you see any mail for me in the hall?"

"No. None whatsoever," I said.

He fell into a humble, whining tone of voice: "Oh, dear, oh, dear. And you say it so triumphantly. You are so pleased that I haven't got any letters. You want to punish me," and he turned his face to the corner and stood there, with his head bent.

I thought, Perhaps he's not a doctor at all. Perhaps he's an actor, impersonating one.

"Come in," he said, "sit down. Take off what you want to take off and leave on what you want to leave on. We'll go out later."

I sat down on the settee, and he brought a chair over and sat down, facing me.

He said, "You always wanted to have long hair but your mother would not let you." He looked at me.

I lowered my head.

He continued: "Then you started to grow it as soon as you left home, didn't you?"

"No, of course not," I said snappishly.

He ignored the rudeness of my tone. "Then when?" he asked.

"Must you really go on with it?" I said.

"Yes, I must," he said; "come on, now. When did you let it grow?"

"When I was married," I said in a voice of resignation, and I curled my lips, hoping to convey to him that I thought him absurd and that it was only due to my exceptionally good nature that I bothered to reply at all.

Again he ignored my impertinence.

"Very well," he said; "as soon as you got married?"

"No," I said.

"How soon after you got married?" he asked.

"After four years."

"I see," he remarked. "And what happened when you had been married for four years?" He was watching me again with that hungry, coldly fascinated air of his, as though lying in wait.

"Nothing happened," I said sulkily.

"When did you walk out on your husband?" he asked.

"About a year after this," I said.

"A year after what?" he asked without taking his eyes off me.

I said: "After I—after—oh, leave me alone."

He leaned over and slapped my arm sharply: "Next time I'll hit harder. Come on. After you what?"

"After—after I didn't let him," I said, holding my arm and turning my head away.

He said, "After four years of marriage you would not let your husband have intercourse with you. Is that it?"

"Yes!" I yelled. "Do you want me to give it to you in triplicate, or what?"

"And after four years of marriage you started to grow your hair."

"Yes," I said. "I've told you already. How often do I have to tell you again?"

He looked at me with a delighted smile. "You say you stopped having intercourse," he remarked, "but you stayed with your husband for another year. Now, why was that?"

"I didn't feel I had the right to clear out, just like that. But then, during the last year he became unbearable. I don't really know why. And so I felt justified in leaving him."

"I see," he said; "you waited till he got unbearable, so that you could leave him with a clear conscience, is that it?"

"Yes," I said.

"You provoked him to be unbearable."

"You are ridiculous," I cried. "I never said that. It's not true."

"Isn't it? What did you think you were doing when you didn't allow him to go to bed with you?"

"Nothing," I said. "I didn't think. Anyway, I didn't do a thing to him. And I did all the cooking and the housework, so there was no reason to be as bloody-minded as he was."

"But don't you realise that this is a dreadful thing to do?" he said. "Don't you realise that it is dreadful for a man if he can't make love to his wife?"

"I never thought about it," I said, "I really didn't. Honestly."

"You needn't say 'honestly' to me," he remarked. "I'll decide for myself about this honesty of yours."

"This is too much," I said, getting up. "Do you think I'm lying, or what? I wouldn't take the trouble to lie to you. You are not worth lying to, with all the beastly questions you ask. And when I say it's true, then it's true. After all, I should know my own thoughts, if anybody does."

"Sit down. And don't talk such rubbish," he said. "How can you know your own thoughts? You don't even know where they come from. You can't even control them. You can't even control your own memories."

I sat down again.

His questions were of the same nature as his love-making had been—insistent, probing, painfully unpleasant, and they made me feel helpless.

"In what way did your husband become unbearable?" he asked.

I said, "Oh, brutal fits of temper, completely out of the blue. For no reason at all."

"For no reason at all," he repeated, adding, "And what did he do in those fits of temper?"

I said disdainfully, "He'd get up from the table and give it a shove, and upset all the plates and dishes, and spill everything, and there'd be a mess on the cloth and on the carpet. And once he threw ink at me. And once I locked myself into the bathroom, and he wanted to come in, to wash his hands. Which he could have done at the kitchen sink. So there was really no need for it. And yet I was frightfully polite, really; I told him I'd open in two minutes; but he broke the door through. It was always after—when he tried to and I wouldn't let him. Once he got hold of me and ripped my blouse and tore off my sleeve. And that's when I had enough, what with the clothes rationing and everything."

"You got pleasure out of refusing him and seeing him distressed," he said, smiling.

"No, I didn't," I cried. "It gave me no pleasure at all. All I wanted was to get out and away. And I never said anything to provoke him when he started to rave. I was awfully well behaved. I shut up and left the room. I did not even slam the door."

"You were as provocative as you knew how to be," he said, still smiling. "The not-slamming made it even worse."

"Don't be ridiculous," I said, "but you know—it's funny, really, even when he was violent, I wasn't afraid of him. He couldn't scare me. Ever."

"And you hated him, didn't you?" he asked lightly.

"I never hated him," I said.

"Dear little woman," he remarked, "I should have thought you'd hate him."

"You really are more stupid than I imagined."

"So you were too kind to hate him, is that it?"

I remained silent.

He leaned forwards and took hold of my wrist. "Tell me," he said.

I shook my head.

He turned my wrist. The pain made me gasp. "Stop it," I said.

"Tell me. Why didn't you hate him?" he asked.

"Because . . ." I said, and feeling the tightening of his hard fingers over my pulse, I added, "because you can't hate somebody when you despise him."

"That's better," he said. He released me. "First you provoked

48

him into violence and then you despised him because it didn't get him anywhere. That's about it, isn't it?"

"Yes, I suppose that's true," I said sullenly.

He said, "I don't suppose. I know. And that's when you decided to walk out. And that's when you started to grow your hair long."

"Did I?" I said. I was astonished.

"You told me so yourself," he remarked, leaning back in his chair and watching me coldly and intently.

I felt both pleased and resentful. Pleased, because his greed in questioning me betrayed an interest which I found flattering. Resentful, because I was, against my will, giving him something of myself with which I would never have parted if I could have helped it. Now my resentment gained the upper hand.

"So what?" I said. "Why do you keep harping on it? What's my walking out got to do with growing my hair long?"

"You rebelled against your mother," he said, looking amused again; "you broke your marriage, which was something your mother would not have approved of—"

"But she couldn't stop me," I cried. "For one thing, I was in England and she wasn't, and I couldn't write home because of the war, letters were cut off, and anyway—even if she'd been here, she couldn't have stopped me."

"Exactly," he said. "You decided once and for all to get rid of your mother. You grew your hair as a gesture of defiance and emancipation. You did something your mother had not allowed you to do when you were a little girl. Your mother. Your mother."

"I've been waiting for this," I said, tilting my head back and giving him a haughty look from beneath lowered lashes. "With you it's throw the cat no matter how, it will always land on its four paws. Doesn't anything else ever occur to you? Do you always have to come back to my mother?"

Again he ignored the insulting vein of my words.

"My poor child," he said, "something else does occur to me, but I can't afford it yet. I've got to keep you in a good mood."

"And you are succeeding very well, too," I said crossly.

"Then, you are not in a good mood?" he asked with a delighted smile.

"No, I'm not," I said, still further put out by his pleasure.

He rose from his chair and joined me on the settee. "Come here, my poor child," and he lifted me on to his knees; but he did not take me into his arms. He merely closed his hands round my hips to keep me steady. He said, "You are my little girl. You are my very own little girl."

"You are being ridiculous," I said, fighting against a sense of well-being that invaded me.

"I've always wanted to have a little girl just like you and now I've got you."

I put my head on his chest and closed my eyes. "You are my own little girl," he repeated. I felt marvellously at peace and flooded with gratitude. I raised my head and looked at him. I found his eyes fastened on me with a look of calculating attention.

"Are you comforted now?" he asked.

"I don't need any comforting," I said, and put my face against his shoulder to hide myself from his sight. I was ashamed. I did not want him to see how well he had succeeded.

"No, no, of course not," he said soothingly.

"And I'm not a little girl," I said.

"No, of course not," he said.

"And I'm grown-up," I said, pressing closer against him.

"Of course you are grown-up," he said. "I can feel how grown-up you are, and if you hadn't so much on, I could feel it still more. Now go and make loo-loo and then we'll go out," and he stretched his legs out in front of him so that I slid off his knees.

"Yes," I said, and went to the bathroom.

It was a warm, sunny day again, and he took me for a walk in Regent's Park.

He told me about life in a hospital in North Africa during the war and what a desperate scarcity of women there had been. "I thought myself most lucky," he said, "that I got hold of a nurse at all. Most lucky. And then, afterwards, she came over here and wanted to see me and I had to take her out. In my despair I took her walking through the park. Just as I'm taking you now," and he turned to look at me.

"I got it; you needn't rub it in," I said, laughing.

"And I wouldn't have minded the walk so much," he continued, "but I had to listen to her talk. It was painful. She'd say things like, do look at that little doggie over there. Just a stupid woman."

"But what's the difference," I said, "if she says, look at that little doggie? That's just as interesting as my long hair. It's both rot. And doesn't add up to anything." And I thought that I wouldn't mind about my long hair so much if at least he'd say that it was lovely. Even the most imbecile Major Carter would have remarked on it by now. But not he. Heaven forbid.

I said, "You could have started pestering her about the little doggie, for instance. Why she liked it. That would have given you something to talk about in your beastly way."

"You don't like my questions, do you?"

"No."

"Why don't you?"

"Because you dig and dig and it's uncomfortable."

"You don't know the pleasure you are giving me. My sweet child," he remarked.

I glanced at him. I was bewildered.

Then I remembered something I had wanted to ask.

"What sort of hospital was it you talked about just now?" I said. "What are you, really?"

"I'm a psychiatrist," he said.

"Oh," I said. "I've never met a psychiatrist before." My heart had given a leap when he had said it. There was something sinister about him after all. I was right. He looked it and was it. It's a sinister job, messing about with people's souls. And glancing at him sideways, I said, "If Goethe had written his *Faust* today, he'd have made Mephisto into a psychiatrist."

"Is that how it strikes you?" he said, with a smile of deep amusement.

"Yes," I said, "but I know nothing about it, of course. I've really no idea."

"Of course you haven't," he said. "People don't. They say to me, you take the bricks off, piece by piece, and then you put them together again. Or they say, you go into the labyrinth and slay the Minotaur. That's all rubbish. They can't understand. How could they?"

"But you are not so idiotic with your patients the way you are with me?" I asked.

"No, my poor child," he said, "I promise you."

"But I mean," I said, "yesterday you said you'd want to go on and on about my long hair. I think we've had it, today. Really. You'll stop now, won't you?"

He said, "You think life is like passing an exam. You get a good mark. Or a bad mark. And that's the end of it. But it isn't. You are your own examiner and it always goes on. It never stops."

I felt a chill of fear and apprehension run through me. I halted and turned to him. He stopped, too. We looked at each other.

"Well?" he asked.

I did not speak.

"You don't like me, do you?" he said.

"No," I said.

"Yes, I know. My sweet child."

We resumed our walk in silence till he made me laugh by saying, "Do look at that little doggie over there."

Later on, we went to a pub in Park Road and had dinner at a restaurant in Baker Street. Again he ordered without asking me what I would prefer, and again I submitted to his highhandedness with a feeling of gratification. I was altogether in a peaceful, dreamy, non-quarrelsome mood, and I did not even flare up when, upon my remarking that I could not eat any more, he told me to finish the piece of roast beef on my plate and that I could leave the rest, though this had certainly never happened to me before when being taken out to dinner.

When we went back to his room and he told me to undress and go to bed, I was still in my docile mood, and I lay down on my back. Yet, as soon as he got near me, my docility was exhausted, and I again made difficulties and resisted yielding my body. When he took possession of me, he did not hurt me, though he again took me endlessly, with the slow-paced inexorable determination of the long-distance runner, and for the whole of the next day my lips and the edges of my inside were so badly bruised that they felt as though they had been rubbed with sand-paper.

As it turned out, this attitude of mine, when being approached by him, never altered, and on most occasions I was driven to struggle and to resist, which was, of course, quite senseless, because I always had to surrender, and I knew I would have to.

But he did not always give me the chance to resist, in the same way as had happened on the first occasion, on the bench in the garden.

Sometimes, when he opened the door to me and I stepped inside, he would make a harmless remark, like asking me about the mail or whether it had stopped raining, and while I was answering, he slid one arm between my legs and the other round my waist, lifted me up, laid me on the hall floor and took possession of me there and then.

One evening, when I was particularly sulky after having been subjected to his uncomfortable questions about "my long hair," he said at last with one of his horribly cheerful crocodile's grins: "Very well, I'll let you off now. We'll go out and drink our heads off."

I was waiting for him in the hall when he called me back: "Come here, my poor child. And take your gloves off. Something's just occurred to me."

I returned to the room.

He made me sit down and show him my hands.

"Do you know, last night I had dinner with Dr. Crombie," he said, "and when the maid came round with the dishes, I looked at her hands and they were full of scabies."

"What's that got to do with me?" I asked. "That's Dr. Crombie's concern."

I was by then quite familiar with Dr. Crombie's name. He was a colleague of Gordon's, a psychiatrist of the same school as Gordon; he was Scottish like Gordon, and he was a native of a village near Glasgow, only five miles distant from the one Gordon came from. Crombie was Gordon's guardian angel, friend, and patron-saint. He was somewhat older than Gordon, held many official appointments, and was feeding Gordon with dinners, patients, and consultant jobs. When, in view of this, I had once remarked, "Crombie must think a great deal of you, *mirabile dictu*," Gordon had said, "Don't talk rubbish. It's got nothing to do with that. It's only because we are nearly from the same village."

Now, confronted with the gratuitous tale of Crombie's maid and her affliction, and being eager to get away for drinks, I added, "Anyway, I think he's awfully lucky to have a maid with scabies. Much better than none without it. Let's go, shall we?" And rose.

"Not so fast," said Gordon. "What's this you've got on your hand?"

"That's a scratch," I said, "and I haven't got scabies, if that's what you mean."

"This is the way people always talk," said Gordon, "and what if it is?" And falling into a querulous, maundering cockney voice, he went on, "And what if I catch it from you, and have to go to hospital and then they ask me how I got it and I'd have to say I've been intimate with a lady, and be ashamed something cruel. You've no consideration for me, you'd sell me down the street, that's what you are all like, you women, all over, and no good to any decent Christian."

I laughed, and he said, "Sit down, and I'll get my magnifying glass."

I sat down on the settee; he rose, tipped me over backwards, and was inside me.

There were times when he hurt me, and times when he did not, and I could never make out whether he hurt me purposely or whether it was accidental.

Sometimes I felt so defiant in my humiliation at having to submit that I bit my teeth together and kept silent. Sometimes I could not control myself and moaned and whimpered, and sometimes I got enraged and yelled, "No, no, I can't stand it. Stop it."

And though on some of these occasions he would ignore my protests and outcries, there were other times when he would say, "Ah, that's good. This is so good. Oh, I know when I'm well off," and he slowed down his pace and drove himself still more deeply inside me, with a deliberate, slow, greedy determination, in the way one eats caviare in small spoonfuls in order to make it last longer, till I fell into a state of darkness, of dissolution, of loss of my being, when I was so completely at his mercy that I only existed to receive him, and if he had not been inside me I could have melted away into nothingness.

My grandmother had a saying, "There are people who have to be forced to their happiness"; and every time he dominated me against my will and forced me to accept the pain he inflicted on me, and not to fight it, he made me feel angry and ashamed.

Yet, above and beyond these emotions, he filled me with a deep extraordinary happiness and satisfaction which I had never known before. It was like the commonplace experience of taking off in a plane in bad weather, flying first into a sheet of thick clouds and then rising still higher into the clear sky and brilliant sunshine. When he possessed me so fiercely that he drove me to the brink of darkness, he gave me the ecstasy of knowing that I had reached the one thing, the only thing, I had ever wanted.

When he was about to take me, I was yearning for him to shatter me and to break me down, and perhaps this was the reason why I made difficulties. Perhaps I put up this defence in order to provoke him to shatter and to break. But at the same time, my resistance had another, a different meaning. I was also longing to shatter him and to break him down. Each time we lay together, I was hoping to achieve it and to drag him into my darkness, and each time, when I regained my senses and opened my eyes and found him clad in his dressing gown and moving about the room quite unconcernedly, I felt a fury of disappointment which, in turn, added depth to my delicious feeling of defeat.

I began to hate his dressing gown. It was of dark green glossy silk woven with a pattern of metallic gold dragons. He had told me he bought it in Japan, during his year's voyage as ship's doctor. It was a flamboyantly gorgeous piece and utterly in contrast with his discreet, unobtrusive Savile Row suits. No decent man, I felt, had business to own such a garment; a decent man had a dressing gown of pure silk, of course, but of soft foulard, either dark blue or burgundy red, and patterned in the tiny squares, dots, or the medallions peculiar to neckties. The golden dragons glittering on the dark background were to me an insult. They stressed, with their brilliant gaudiness, his mastery over me.

Apart from the fact that I could not tell whether he hurt me on purpose or not, it was a mystery how it was done at all, because my own position never varied. He always made me lie down on my back with my thighs resting, slightly apart, on the sheet, and if I ever so much as raised my knee he would force it down again, and if I twisted sideways he would bring me back to being spread out flat. And moreover, what I understood least of all was why no other man had ever penetrated me so far and so painfully.

I never once undressed on my own initiative. He always had to tell me, "Undress and lie down." When I had found his questions about my hair particularly disturbing, I became defiant and said, "No, why should I? Go to hell," and then it happened that he dragged me by my hair so that I could not get away, and undid the hooks and buttons of my blouse and skirt, tore open the zip-fastener of my corsets and peeled those off together with my stockings, giving me orders like "Lift your arm now" and "Step out of your shoes" in the voice of someone going through with a wearisome task, and concluding with a remark of feigned self-pity, such as "God, the trouble you are giving me." But on other such occasions, when I told him to go to hell, he would merely say in a low voice of barely contained rage, "Take it off before I tear it off," and then I hurriedly obeyed.

The only times when I behaved with exceptional submissiveness were on some evenings when we had been having drinks after dinner. Upon returning to his room, he would say with heavily acted joviality, "Now, come and undress, my poor child. No sex and no cruelty, of course," and then I stripped off my clothes speedily and lay down on the bed with my thighs apart the way he wanted it, and observing me, he said, "Now you are good. You are so sweet when you are good," and he approached the bed, saying, "It takes two gins to make a normal woman out of you," and plunged straight into me.

Yet I must avoid giving the misleading impression that he only did this when I was "being good." He always plunged straight into me, without fondling or caressing me, whether I was willing or unwilling, as soon as I was in the position he wanted. Gordon never came anywhere near me with his hands or his lips, as though this would have been a weakness on his part, a superfluous gesture of unnecessary contact. And it was this total abstention from all caresses, this paring down of all that was needless from possessing me, this deliberate withholding of tenderness, which added to my mortification.

And just as he treated me as I had never been treated by a lover before, I also behaved in a manner devoid of making him welcome, never folding my arms around his neck, never stroking him or gentling him either.

It was not only my feeling of truculence which drove me to this, the feeling of "If you are this way, I'll be hanged if I'll be otherwise," but also another emotion: that it would be an unforgivable act of sacrilege, of *lèse-majesté,* of profanation, if I ever touched his virility. This conviction that I must never reach out to him and touch his forbidden places even went so far that I never once, fully and properly, saw his sex. When he walked to the bed, naked, from the far end of the room, I might glance at him sideways and see that he desired me, and then quickly avert my eyes.

I went still further than that. I could not even bring myself to call him by his Christian name of Richard. I never called him anything, just "you," when talking to him. When I was alone, thinking of him, I called him Gordon.

He was somewhat better in this respect, but only apparently so; he called me "my poor child," and more rarely, "my sweet child," but I did not conceive this as an expression of tenderness; it was patronising, it was the mark of his superiority over me. He was the owner and I was the slave. He never once called me by my name, Louisa, and why should he have done so? One also calls "waiter" and "porter" without bothering to find out that those helpful and necessary creatures are named Dick or Harry.

When I spent the second night in his room, he did not, as I have said, hurt me. And as time went on, I divided his love-making into these two kinds, when it hurt and when it did not.

The kind when it did not hurt was at first much more ordinary, apart from its exceedingly long duration—more similar to shorter experiences with other men, though only Gordon could impart to me that exquisite feeling of helplessness, of being fastened to him irrevocably, of not being able to get away. But then, perhaps after six weeks of being his mistress, and at first only when I had had two gins, I began to open up and receive him avidly, with sensations of bliss which dawned and unfolded in those deep regions of which I had only become aware at first by the pain he inflicted on me. This was nothing like the sharp flickering climax I had reached so quickly when he had laid me over the edge of the bench in his garden. I was pervaded by a marvellous sweetness which streamed through me, and its spreading flow would have made me willing, as Faust was, to let such a fleeting moment of fulfillment be his last, saying, *"Werd ich zum Augenblicke sagen, verweile doch, du bist so schön, dann sollst du mich in Fesseln schlagen, dann will ich gerne mit dir gehn,"* when he made his pact with Mephisto.

Chapter

Three

Gordon never mentioned the fact that he was my lover, and I, too, never alluded to it.

He did, though, often talk about erotic subjects in general, shocking me, and remarking sarcastically, "We psychiatrists are disgusting. Everything reminds us of sex. Even when we are in bed with a naked woman, we think of sex."

One afternoon, when I came in, he gave me a book I had lent him. I had done this several times before, in an endeavour to educate him as, to my mind, he was deplorably ignorant of literature. Usually he would return the book with a taunt which both vexed and amused me, such as when, regarding *Death in Venice*, he said, "I suppose Thomas Mann does show some promise, after all."

The book he returned to me on that day was the bible of the *fin-de-siècle* decadence, Huysmans's *À Rebours,* and to my amazement, it turned out that he was delighted with it; he started to talk about it as soon as I entered the room. While I listened, I realised how little of *À Rebours* I had, myself, understood, and how his judgment, compared to mine, was like an X-ray picture compared to a photograph.

After having lifted out the skeleton of Huysmans's psychology, Gordon went on to say that the book contained the description of a dream which, in any case, was so excellent, that for this alone the work would have been worth reading.

"What's so special about it?" I asked.

"Don't say 'special,' say 'especial,' " he said.

"Yes," I said.

"It is the classical fear of the vagina dentata," he said.

I was taken aback, not certain of the meaning, but certain enough to be shocked.

"How do you mean?" I asked. "It's got teeth, or what?"

"Don't you know it?" he said. "No, I suppose you don't, my poor child. It's like that magazine, *For Men Only*. It's the man's fear of the woman. The woman has teeth inside her and when he gets in, she will bite his penis off and cripple him."

"I never heard anything like it," I said.

"I am disgusting, am I not?" he asked.

"Yes," I said, "not only disgusting, but worse. I don't know where you get your ideas from."

"Oh, dear, oh, dear, now I have to be punished again. Oh, dear, what have I done to deserve it?" he exclaimed in the shrill voice of the rejected lover, which always made me laugh. "By the way," he continued, "an ex–army captain came to see me today. And he was only like this"—and his face became convulsed by a violent and complicated twitching, involving one eye and one side of the mouth—"but he was much better than he used to be," and he looked at me, as though greatly surprised by my laughter. "I didn't take him," he added. "I didn't fancy him. But you know, my Maltese is blossoming out," and falling into a rasping basso voice: "Doctor, I like a slim boy with a big cock. But, doctor, it's not sex, it's aesthetic," and as I shrieked with laughter, he continued, "What he actually likes is to get hold of a couple of such aesthetic boys and squeeze in between them."

"Incredible," I said, stunned.

"Ah, that's what you say," he remarked, "but heaven knows what you do with yourself when you are out of my sight."

I laughed again, but this time my laughter was forced.

"Oh, don't be silly," I said, lowering my head.

If he meant what I thought he meant, then he was wrong. I had not done so since I had met him. I had no desire of it and, even if I had wanted to, I would not have dared, for fear he might have guessed it. His knowledge of it would have embarrassed me unbearably, though he probably would have considered it with the same amusement with which he contemplated the bizarre aberrations of his patients. So far so good. But apart from this, my conscience was not clear and I told myself defiantly that there were realms of my life which he would not enter, despite his digging and delving.

As though reading the former part of my thought, he said, wandering away from me and moving towards the window, "Playing with yourself is a sorry business," and when I remained silent, he repeated, "A very sorry business," still with his back turned to me. Then he wheeled round on his heels and added, while stepping up to the desk, his eyes lowered, as though searching for something among his papers, "It's the one horrible, unspeakable sin. Time after time, with every patient, up it comes with the monotonous regularity of a cracked gramophone record." He raised his eyes, and by that time I had stopped feeling flustered and could afford to meet his glance with the righteousness of injured innocence.

"Really," I said, "how interesting."

My steady glance was not the success I had promised myself. He was watching me with a calculating eye.

"What are you afraid of?" he asked.

"Nothing," I said.

"Have you ever been afraid of a man before?" he asked.

"No," I said.

"Why are you afraid of me?"

"Because—" I began. I thought, He doesn't know and I'm not going to tell him. I'll be hanged if I do. And then looking at him and thinking, He does have queer eyes, I said, improvising recklessly, "Because of your eyes. You've got such unpleasant eyes. So piercing and penetrating."

"I see," he said, "and you are afraid I might find out something about you with my piercing and penetrating eyes?"

"No, of course not," I said; "there's nothing to—"

"I see," he said.

For a while we remained silent. I watched him as he paced the room. He halted and gave one of his horribly inviting grins. "Now, what shall we do about it?" he said, leaning against the desk.

"Do what about what?" I asked.

"About your being afraid of me," he said. "Do I seem to you like a monster? Are you inferring that I'm a monster?"

"I never said that," I exclaimed.

"Fiddlesticks," he remarked. "And now that you said so, I'd better live up to it," and he slowly advanced towards me.

I could not control the fear which gripped me. I dashed round him in a semi-circle and got behind the desk. "You are not going to hit me," I cried.

He turned to me with a delighted countenance.

"Oh, is that what you want?" he said.

"No, of course not. You are silly," I exclaimed. I was on the verge of tears and kept holding on to the edge of the desk.

He looked calm and agreeable.

I let go of the desk. "You really are silly," I said, feeling relieved. I took a deep breath to steady myself.

He had been acting a part, as he so often did; only it had been a part he had never assumed before. Yet, though I realised the absurdity of my fright, I could not understand it, and I could not laugh it off.

"Yes, that was a good dream in this book," he said. He started again to pace the room. I sat down in the chair by the desk. "Men are peculiar creatures, you know," he continued; "most of the time they spend worrying if they are as well equipped as their fathers. Or they adore Jesus. He's the man with all the magic—there's no woman he can't make. Then they develop kinks like the one I told you about and work up a grudge against women. They squander on her the seed, the most precious stuff they've got, the priceless liquid." And falling into the voice of a whining cockney, he added, "Yes, there you go, laughing, and we poor men are getting thinner and weaker, while you are feeding on us and getting fatter all the time. You are dreadful, you women." He stopped in his tracks. "How does this strike you?" he asked.

"I don't know anything about it," I said, curling my lips. "I suppose you are right."

"Ah, yes," he said, "you think I am like the Bible, do you? Verily, verily, I say unto you, and if it were not so I would not say so?"

I smiled.

"Why don't you tell me one of your dreams sometime?" he said.

"No," I said.

"Why not?" he asked. "Are you afraid of what might come out?"

"I've got nothing to hide," I said.

"Not much," he said. "You are trying to run away from me all the time."

I said, "Because your patients are cracked and full of filth, you imagine everybody else is the same, too. But I'm not. I'm normal."

He considered me gravely for a while. "Yes," he said, "you are fairly normal."

"And I'm quite simple and straightforward," I said.

"No. You are very complicated, very complicated indeed," he said, and, to my astonishment, he made it sound like praise.

"Anyway," I said saucily, "if I'm fairly normal, what do you want with my dreams?"

"It gives me tremendous pleasure dealing with you," he said, "getting things out of you against your will. I like to pierce you and penetrate you unpleasantly. Oh, yes, my poor child."

I looked at him. Then I turned my face away. Beyond my upset I was flooded by a deep happiness, similar to the one he made me feel when forcing me to surrender to his virility. No one else before him had given me this gratification, but I realised now that the longing to be violated, body and soul, must have always been inside me.

When I was sixteen, and still at school, one of my class-mates got married, and the story got round that on the wedding night the bridegroom had used her so brutally that she had been sent to hospital the next day to be stitched up. All the girls in my form, and their mothers, professed their horror and disgust at the tale. And yet, at the time, it had filled me with an envious desire which I kept to myself and drove me to wonder how many of the others were secretly feeling the same. I do not think that such longings are unusual. If they were, the cinema, which lives on people's immoral yearnings, would not show so many near-rapes.

It was as though I had been in possession of one of those small shells with Japanese flowers which are sold at street corners. When plunged into a bowl of water, the tightly sealed shell opens and the flat, dry, coiled-up, insignificant shreds of paper contained within float out and unfold their variegated and unsuspected splendor; with Gordon I had found my bowl of water.

Chapter

Four

Shortly after this, I did not see Gordon for a whole week. Usually, I met him about four times a week and spent the whole Sunday with him.

When I saw him again, he gave me no reason and I asked for none either.

Now, in the late afternoon, as we were sitting in a pub in George Street, I was feeling fresh and high-spirited, as he had not yet ground me down with his love-making; I was also nettled over his silence regarding his activities during that last week, when he had felt no desire for my presence.

I said tauntingly, "Isn't it lucky we've met today? Because I had a very unpleasant dream last night. Imagine what you might have missed."

"Tell me," he said.

"I was covered with scarlet cucumber seeds," I said; "they were sticking to my body, and when I rubbed my skin, they all came off, except one that had grown into my arm, and when I pulled it out it left a cup-shaped wound. It was ghastly."

"Really," he said, greatly amused; "cucumber seeds. I didn't know you were so afraid of getting V.D. and getting pregnant and having abortions."

"Of course I am," I said.

"But you shouldn't be," he said, still smiling. "If you want to be free and lead an adventurous life, then you mustn't be afraid. It doesn't go together."

"But I am," I said. "I'm always worried about getting caught and getting a disease. Of course, with you, I don't worry about a disease."

"Why not?" he asked.

"Because you are a doctor," I said.

"I've had syphilis," he said.

"No. You are joking!" I exclaimed.

"Oh, no," and he repeated very slowly and emphatically, "I've had syphilis."

I was so taken aback I did not know what to say.

After a pause he said, "But anyway, V.D. and pregnancies are grown-up fears. That's not what I want from you. It's not the dream I want. You just threw me this as a sop."

I glanced at him sideways. "I did have another one, which I still remember exactly," I said, "but that was some time ago."

"You think it's got to be newly laid, like an egg?" he said; "or, 'Give me ten sixpenny stamps, please, miss, and I hope they are fresh, they're for a friend of mine who is in hospital.' "

I laughed.

"Nothing but evasions," he said.

During the talks about my hair there had arisen similar occasions, when he had got annoyed with me for similar reasons: "You've only said this to distract me," and: "No, that's not what I want—start again at the beginning," and: "You've said this on purpose, to mislead me," and I would never know what was wrong with my replies and what he wanted to hear. It was as though he were asking me to give him all the rubies contained in a jewel case, and I, being colour-blind, kept handing him the emeralds as well.

Apart from this, he was extremely patient with me, and when I

did not want to answer and he slapped my arm or turned my
wrist or tugged at my hair, it was never because he was exasperated with my slowness but only to overcome my reluctance to
disclose what I, to myself, called the "innermost secrets of my
nature." Why I was so unwilling to hand them over, I never
knew. Besides, that appellation of mine, "innermost secrets of
my nature," was quite a mouthful; it was ludicrously and preten-
tiously bombastic and self-important, all the more so as those secrets never boiled down to anything more exciting than that, for
instance, I had been livid with envy at the age of five when my
mother used to come to my room *en grande toilette* to say good
night to me, and that I had wished to go to the opera, too. I had
no secrets which were shameful or dishonourable to disclose; I
was not guilty of any crimes which I might wish to hide; and yet
I resisted and fought before handing to him those pitifully banal
incidents from my past. I dreaded telling them, as though they
were monstrous and atrocious, and I was terrified he would be
revolted upon hearing them.

He was never revolted. He was delighted, and encouraging
and insatiable.

And yet, they were "secrets," strictly speaking, in so far as I
had never before told them to anyone, and also because, sometimes, they were secrets to myself and I had never known they
were inside me, like, for instance, my feelings of hatred against
my mother. I only discovered and admitted this under his probing, and it made me doubly annoyed that I had to hand over to
him what without him I would have never known.

I was at a loss to understand how such trivial incidents, when
recalled, could whirl up such a storm of guilt and shame in me
and how they could assume such an importance. Then, one day, I
came across an Elizabethan poem, composed of two parts; each
verse contained an enumeration of the marvels of the world,

such as Etna spitting fire, the flying fish of the China Sea, and the geysers of Iceland spouting boiling water. Then came the refrain:

> *These things are wondrous,*
> *Yet more wondrous I,*
> *Whose heart with fear doth freeze,*
> *With love doth fry.*

At least somebody who is sincere, I said to myself.

I was still thinking of it when Gordon said, "This is such a really old-fashioned pub. Has it ever struck you about these places?—they have a religious air. The stained-glass windows. And the benches like pews. And the bar like the altar."

"Yes," I said, "now that you say it, I see it. But it's never struck me before."

"And it's never struck me before," he said, "that you are so afraid of getting pregnant," and he looked at me with an amused smile.

That night he did not leave me in order to put on his dressing gown. He remained in bed beside me.

"Well, if you are so worried about a baby, go and do something about it . . . Get up and wash," he said.

"Do you think so?" I asked. "But what with?"

"Just water," he said, and switched on one of his sinister crocodile smiles.

"All right, I'll go," I said, feeling suspicious. I was most doubtful about his advice. It sounded quite inadequate. On the other hand, I was in no position to quarrel with him; he was a doctor.

He was observing me.

"All right, I'll do it," I said, sitting up.

"Why are you in such a hurry?" he asked. "They can't jump."

"I'll go now before it is too late," I said, and put my feet on the floor.

"Don't be so impatient to get away from me," he said.

"I'll go," I said, "and you aren't going to stop me."

"Don't talk such rubbish," he said; "all this I will and you won't and you can't. I can stop you, and you know it."

"No, you can't," I said, standing up and turning away from the bed.

He reached out, grabbed a handful of my hair, and pulled me towards him. I staggered some paces backwards and fell into his lap as he pulled me on to the bed. He bent my arms over my back and held them there, joined together. I braced my shoulders against his chest, leaped like a fish, and kicked out with one leg into the bedside table and set it rocking, together with the lamp, so that the light went flickering on and off with each of my kicks.

But even then, while he used force, I could feel how carefully he was handling me, and I thought bitterly that the only time I was ever in his arms was when he wanted to impose his will.

By the time the light was burning steadily again, he had taken possession of me. After he had come to the end of his pleasure, he said, "Go and wash."

I remained with my eyes closed and shook my head.

"That's better," he said; "and now, stop the nonsense, once and for all."

"Yes," I said.

"My sweet child."

When he saw me home on the following morning, he told me to meet him that day at Shepherds at half past six. Then he asked me, "What did you do with yourself all this week?"

"I had a cold," I said, "so I kept indoors most of the time. I was really quite glad I didn't see you."

"Weren't you miserable, away from me?" he asked.

"If you must know, I was," I said.

"Ah, yes," he said with a grin, "it was a week of chastisement."

"There's no need to be so bloody-minded about it," I said.

He said, "I can afford it. When one has gone through it oneself, one has the right to be frivolous."

"Don't be so conceited," I said, "because I don't—I'm not fond of you."

"I know you aren't," he said, "and that makes it so much worse."

I never found out why he had not wished to see me for that whole week; but it never happened again.

That evening at Shepherds I sat down on the same low windowsill from which he had plucked me when he had first spoken to me, and I looked about me idly while he went to the bar to get our drinks.

When he returned, I said, "There's a man who was in our mess in Hamburg. That's the first time I've seen anybody here from our crowd."

"Which one is he?" he asked.

I pointed him out.

"What's his name?" he asked.

"Major Winthrop," I said.

Gordon left me and I lost sight of him as a group of people came in and blocked my view.

He came back after a short while. "I spoke to him," he said.

"Why on earth?" I asked.

"I just wanted to. I said to him, are you Winthrop? And he said he was. Then I said, I'm here with Mrs. Walbrook, do you want to speak to her? and he said he didn't."

I looked at Gordon. He seemed greatly pleased. "You see, my poor child," he said, "he had no wish to see you."

72

"I'm not surprised," I said snappishly. "He never was in our lot. He had other fish to fry. German girls. Anyway, I hardly knew him."

"It looks like it," said Gordon.

"But why did you speak to him?" I asked.

"I just wondered," said Gordon.

We left soon afterwards and I fell to thinking how Gordon would have behaved if, instead of the indifferent Major Winthrop, it had been, say, Colonel Prior, with whom I had had an affair for two months till I had finished it, to his distress. I had never got any pleasure from him at all, but he had not known it and I had not enlightened him. Instead, I had ended it decently, telling him that despite the precautions I was taking I had been so anxious when my "curse" had come a week too late that I couldn't stand the strain. He had swallowed it.

Yet I never thought about taking precautions during all the time that Gordon was my lover. When I saw him for the second time, I already knew, intuitively, that he would not be "careful" and that he would not have tolerated it if I had tried to be so. I was certain that the man who had said "Don't withdraw from me" and whose thumb in the bend of my elbow had forced me into submission wanted a complete surrender and that there was no chance of compromise.

After the night when I had made the bedside lamp flicker on and off, the subject was never mentioned between us and I did not give it another thought. I knew that if ever the need arose he would deal with it, but I never even wondered whether, in such a case, he would have let me have the child. I never was impregnated by him, which was strange, because I had been pregnant before. And it was bitter, because he was the only man from whom I have ever wanted a child.

Chapter

Five

I never asked Gordon about his past, for the same reason that I did not dare to call him Richard, because he was in control and I was the underling. Even when I was rude to him, and flung insults at him, I did not do so as between equals. I was impertinent and saucy like a maid-servant towards her master. This was as I felt it at the time. I only realised later the true nature of our relationship, which was certainly that of the master and the dependent, but on an entirely different basis.

The little I got to know about his past he told me one afternoon while we were walking in Regent's Park, when we must have known each other for about three months; it was the beginning of September, and the weather was still fine and warm and the grass still dry enough to sit on.

First we had been strolling along the river and had stopped to feed the ducks. That is, Gordon fed the ducks and I stood looking on, watching him more than the ducks. I disapproved of his way of feeding them; he fed them unfairly, letting the more alert ones get the advantage over the sluggish ones, but despite my protests he never allowed me to join him and would not hand me as much as a single crust of bread. When I begged him to let me have some, too, he said, "No, this is child's stuff, and you don't want any. Because you are grown-up, aren't you?"

"Of course I'm grown-up," I said.

"You must be," he said; "you told me you were a grown-up woman the other day, didn't you? So I took your word for it. You would not deceive me, would you?"

"But I want to feed the ducks, too," I said.

"No, my poor child," he said, "not till you admit that you are not grown-up. Will you admit it, now?"

"Over your dead body," I said.

"Truer things have been spoken in jest," he remarked. He threw the empty bag into a litter-bin. "Dead or alive, I'm nothing if not tidy. Come along now," and taking me by the wrist he led me towards the bridge. We crossed and sat down on the other side of the water, on a sloping lawn, in the shelter of some shrubs.

A little boy came running past us and knocked against my foot. I changed my position and arranged my legs differently, and he came dashing back and again knocked against my foot.

I smiled, pretending to be amused.

"Why don't you hit the bugger?" said Gordon. "That's what you want to do, isn't it?"

"Yes," I said, ashamed of myself. Women, when in the company of men, are invariably playing up to the idea men have of them. They pretend to be patient, sweet-tempered, long-suffering, and tender towards all children.

I turned to Gordon and saw that he was watching me with a smile, and once again felt the wonderful relief that I could not and did not need to disguise myself with him and that he accepted me as I was, with all my objectionable qualities.

"All this love for children—I don't know," he said, lying down on his side and supporting himself on an elbow. "I've got a child myself. I've hardly ever seen it. I can't say I feel any love for it."

The child, he told me, was from his marriage. When it was born he was abroad, serving in the army, and his wife had left him a few months after the birth and run off with an American soldier, a lorry driver. Only quite recently Gordon had gone through the final phase of his divorce, and the wife was about to marry the man and go to America, taking the baby with her.

I was careful not to show my surprise, nor to make any comments, for fear of slamming shut the door he was opening into his past. He started to tell me about his wife. She had been a nurse, he said, on the lowest level of normal intelligence, a border-line case edging on mental retardation, and when I looked at him with disbelief, he added with a smile, "Oh, yes, that's the category she belongs to. Whereas you are a superior decadent, you are the salt of the earth."

I shook my head over this doubtful compliment.

He had met her, and to get over his infatuation he had left her and enrolled as ship's doctor on a year's voyage round the world. He only mentioned two countries he had touched. One of them was Japan, where he had bought the hateful dragon-strewn dressing gown. The other was Russia. While they had docked for two days in a northern port, a Russian civilian had come on board, an English interpreter sent by the harbour-master's office, to enquire whether he could be of assistance to the members of the crew.

"I had the fellow in my cabin and offered him a drink and a sandwich. Then he started to talk, in English, of course, and I told him I was Scottish, the same as he. He denied it; he said he was Russian and had never been outside Russia. The longer he talked, the more I was able to pin down his accent, till I told him within a radius of ten miles where he came from. Near Glasgow, the same as Crombie and myself. The more I pinned him down, the angrier he got. He left me in a fury. I have always wondered what kind of fate swept him to that God-forsaken place, and what he had to hide, the poor devil."

"And then?" I asked.

"And then I came back and married her," he said. "It hadn't helped at all. The year round the world was good for nothing." And I was gripped by jealous anguish at the thought of his enslavement to the stupid nurse.

Strangely enough, my jealousy was not appeased when he told me that very soon after the marriage he was sick and tired of her, and that he had been on the point of sending her back to her mother when she found she was pregnant. He joined up and left; she had the child and went off with the American, to Gordon's great relief.

"It's a depressing thought," he remarked, "when you consider how short a woman's span is—and yet, while it lasts, one is chained to the wheel of a stupid woman."

I remained silent and he said, "I don't mean you, my sweet child. You have such a lovely brain. You don't know the pleasure you are giving me."

But these words made my heart swell with bitterness; they meant that I was not stupid and that he was not enchained to me. I would have gladly been a stupid woman; I would have gladly traded my "lovely brain" for one word of appraisal, no matter how banal, about my womanly charms. And I recalled with mortification how, the only time I had sunk so low as to play for such a compliment, I had met with failure.

It had happened during one of the talks about "my long hair." I had told him about my great-grandmother, whom I remembered well. She was eighty-four at the time and I was four years old and I could still feel the disgust her yellow and wrinkled hand had inspired in me when I had been made to say "I kiss your hand" and to kiss it. This great-grandmother had been a dazzling beauty; I possessed two photographs of her as a young woman, and I assured Gordon that she would have been a film star if she had lived in our present time.

But unfortunately—and here I started playing for praise—with each generation the family looks had diminished. My grandmother was a beauty, too, but less brilliantly so than my great-grandmother. My mother, though not beautiful, was enchantingly pretty. Then there was me, once more watered-down, looking the way I was, though the family looks had remained basically the same. I refrained from describing them; the thick hair of brownish-black colour, the long oriental eyes which were light brown but appeared dark because they were heavily fringed with black lashes, the smooth pallor, the oval face, the small full mouth and the small perfectly rounded chin. I was hoping that Gordon would perceive what I failed to convey.

And while I was waiting for him to tell me at last—at last—that I was lovely, he said, with a smile, "You are not so bad yourself," and then, turning on me the look of cold, hungry fascination, he asked, "When you started with your great-grandmother, you meant the line on your mother's side, didn't you?"

And when I said, crossly, "Yes, of course," he smiled with satisfaction. He added, "You've remembered it remarkably well, too, I must say," while I, foiled in my purpose, wished I had never embarked on the whole pointless rigmarole.

Now, sitting on the grass beside him, I turned away from him, endeavouring to hide my sadness, and busied myself with plucking a few blades and twisting them round my fingers, when he said, "I've got another child, too. Now, this will amuse you."

I turned towards him but did not raise my eyes, and started to weave the blades into a chain, adding link by link with knotted loops.

A never-ending supply of nurses, I thought, after he had started to talk.

It was yet another of those dedicated and accommodating creatures, employed at that time in the same hospital as he. He did not dwell on the nature of his relationship beyond saying that she had sent for him one night when he was asleep and not on duty, and had asked him to sit by her bed. She was in labour pains. She informed him that the child to be born was his, and he had not contradicted her; it was, he had to admit, a possibility. When the child appeared, he knew it was really his—"It was a black-haired bastard, all right"—and the mother, while being surrounded by the nurses who attended her, took a ring from her handbag, put it on her finger, and announced that she was Mrs. So-and-So, that she had got married some time ago and had wanted to keep it as a surprise.

"How odd," I said. "Why did she do it?"

"You tell me," said Gordon.

"As a revenge," I said. "She was safe, but she didn't want to let you off without a fright."

"Fun and games," he remarked.

It struck me, as it had struck me before, that all the stories which he called "amusing" were based on injury and pain, just as the incident with the pick-pocket in the club in Brook Street had been painful. Fun and games for him were diversions of the same kind as watching trapeze artists who carry on a constant flirtation with death.

"I wonder what you will do to me, one day," he remarked.

"Don't be ridiculous," I said. "Do you imagine I'm like that nurse with a dramatic last-minute wedding ring, or what?"

"Oh, no, you are not as crude as that," he said; "but nevertheless, I can't help wondering."

"Then do the wondering by yourself and to yourself," I said

79

crossly. "You get me quite depressed with that idiotic talk of yours."

"Fiddlesticks," he said, "you are not depressed. You don't know the meaning of the word. What you mean is, you get fed up, or browned off, as you call it."

I remained silent, plaiting my grass chain.

He went on, "And yet, I am so kind to you. Don't you think I am kind? I feed you and buy you drinks and pleasure you, and here I am, a highly skilled man, listening to your girlish babbling. Just like a kind father."

I sat up straight, flung down the grass chain and bit my teeth together.

"Why are you so put out?" he asked. "I'm actually old enough to be your father. I am forty-eight, twenty years older than you are."

"I know. But I've never thought of it that way. Can't we go and have drinks yet?"

He said, "Yes, we can, my poor child. I'll spare you for the time being," and changing to the querulous cockney voice, "Anything to humour a woman. Ah, you are dreadful, you women."

I tilted my face up to him. "I'm sorry," I said.

"Why?" he asked.

"Because I'm so bad-tempered," I said; "but you know, I've never been bad-tempered. And I've never flared up. It's only since I met you—I don't know—I don't understand it."

"Yes, I know," he said, "and of course you don't. You can't understand it. But I do. It's quite all right."

"Then you are not cross with me?" I asked. "I'd be terribly cross with me if I were you."

"I'm not cross," he said; "you are a sheer joy to me. Now come, give me your chain. Did you make it for me?"

"Yes," I said.

"And will you tell me the dream you've been withholding from me?"

"Yes," I said.

"My sweet child."

Chapter

Six

Gordon told me he was invited for the following evening at Dr. Crombie's and I should come to his place the day after that at six o'clock.

I had, by then, made up a clear picture of what Dr. Crombie looked like, though Gordon had never furnished me with any description.

Dr. Crombie was six feet tall. He was round-faced, beefy, short-necked, red-cheeked, easily roused to anger. He had a pug-nose, small suspicious eyes, and was chill, rigid, and standoffish in his bearing. He disdained argument, being certain that he was always in the right. He liked flattery, though pretending to be impervious to it. This image rose in my mind for all the years to come whenever I thought of Dr. Crombie.

Then there was the nurse of the "look at the little doggie." She was a good-natured, buxom young woman with thick calves and heavy thighs; dark-haired, moon-faced, and with coarse, large-pored skin.

The nurse of the wedding ring was fairish, thin of face and body, had long sharp features and an underhung jaw. Her eyes were brilliant and bulging.

The only one whose portrait I never attempted was Gordon's wife. Gordon had made it abundantly clear that she was, for him, finished and done with. And yet the very thought of her was too painful for me to contemplate, because she represented for me the force of sheer senseless, inexplicable, erotic attraction, and therefore I locked her faceless figure away into the jealousy-compartment of my heart. This compartment I liked to imagine as an irrational, crazy room—octagonal, Victorian Gothic, without doors and windows, lined with mirrors which not only multiplied but magnified and glorified the person imprisoned therein, and pervaded, appropriately, by the musty, damply-dusty and mildewy air peculiar to such a place. It was, I knew, unreasonable of me to feel jealous of her the way I did, but this did not diminish the poignancy of my feeling. It was at this time that I began to grasp Pascal's famous utterance: *"Le coeur a ses raisons que la raison ne connaît point."* Up till then I had never been bewildered by my emotions and had always found them reasonable.

I had hoped that Gordon might have forgotten about my promise to tell him the dream, but when, as soon as I arrived, he motioned me to the settee and said, "Let's have it," I did not pretend to be at a loss as to what he meant. I only went as far as to say, "It's quite short. And nothing, really," and he replied, "We'll see."

I said, "It was in the lounge of the Belgrave Park Hotel. I was there, and there was a man whom I know. But he didn't see me. He was with a woman, who was exactly like him, but not like a man disguised as a woman . . . I mean, she could have been his sister. He is outstandingly good-looking and sophisticated and elegant, and he looked just the way he always does. But she, that sister, was terribly frumpish and dowdy, and as tall and lean and angular as he is, most unfortunate for a woman to be. And it was pathetic, because she had obviously tried so hard to smarten herself up; she even had on a hat with a veil. A short veil, very dressy, but it looked pitiful on her. All the time I thought, If only he doesn't see me, or he'll get annoyed with me, that I'm spying on him and trying to find out his secrets, and yet I kept sitting there, in my corner, watching him talking to that woman. Suddenly he looked up and saw me. I was stunned with fright. . . . That's all. You see, it doesn't add up to much."

Gordon had been sitting facing me and listening, with his chin in his hand and looking into space. He remained silent for a while and then said, without shifting his pose, "This man. You say it's a man you know. For how long have you known him?"

"For four years," I said, "but not really. I mean, I met him and then for three years I didn't see him, and all the time I was not sure who he was and if he really was what he'd told me. I mean, before, when I first met him, he'd given me his name, but all the time I thought it probably wasn't his real name. Then I found out it was."

Gordon said, "You say it's a man you know. That's for my benefit, isn't it? You are really very much involved with this man."

I thought, Why does he have to use such ugly words? Involved. Romeo got involved with Juliet: "These things are wondrous, yet more wondrous I, whose heart with fear doth freeze, with involvement doth fry."

"Yes," I said, "I am—he is—the love of my life."

"I see," said Gordon. He paused. "How old is he?" he asked.

"I don't know," I said. "When I first met him, during the war, he looked like a really young man. He's the handsomest man I've ever seen in my life."

"I didn't ask you what he looked like," said Gordon, "I asked you how old he was."

"I don't know," I said, "he's never told me flat out. And it's difficult to say because he wears make-up. He's not effeminate at all, though, he's a film actor. Actors do, you know." And I slipped out of my shoes and curled my legs under me, as I often did when I was on the settee.

"Put your legs down and sit up properly," said Gordon in a voice bleached and tightened with rage.

I put my feet on the floor and sat up straight.

"How old is he?" he asked. "You say you don't know. But you have a pretty good idea about it."

"Well," I said, "from the way he talked about pre-war days, and what he'd done and where he'd been, in the twenties, and so on, for instance—"

"Come on," said Gordon, in a voice still edged with rage.

"He says he has eternal youth and beauty," I said defiantly.

"Yes, with make-up," said Gordon.

"But he does look marvellous," I said.

"So you say," said Gordon.

I said sulkily, "He must have been at least fifty when I met him first."

"That's better," said Gordon. He continued silent for a while. Then he said, "Now, tell me. The first time you met him, did you go to bed with him?"

"No, of course not," I said resentfully.

"Why 'of course not'?" he asked.

"I don't know. It just didn't arise."

"But he was so beautiful?" said Gordon.

"Yes, even so," I said. "Somehow—I didn't—I was just thrilled by his company."

"And then, you say, you met him a year ago," remarked Gordon. "How was that? In Germany?"

"No," I said, "in London. While I was on leave."

"And then you did sleep with him, didn't you?" he said.

"Yes, but only once," I said.

"Why was this?" he asked. "Didn't you want to any more?"

"Of course I did," I cried; "very much."

"Why 'of course, very much'?" asked Gordon; "before, it was 'of course not.' "

"I don't know," I said. "Anyway, it wasn't possible to do more. I had to get back to Hamburg the next day. My leave was up."

"And now, you are seeing him pretty often," said Gordon.

"Yes," I said.

"But altogether, in all those years, you've slept with him only once," remarked Gordon.

"How do you know?" I said, flaring up. "I just told you I'm seeing a lot of him, all the time."

"True," said Gordon; "but when you came to London now, for good, in June, you got into my clutches straightaway. And I've kept you on a very short lead since, my poor child."

I said, "That still doesn't mean that I don't—with him. Sometimes you don't see me for two days."

"Fiddlesticks," he said. "I only have to look at the rings under your eyes and I know what they come from. You mark so strongly, it's there to see even for the whole of the next day."

I said, "You don't know anything, and I can do what I want."

"We've had all this before," said Gordon. "Don't come to me with this rubbish, what you will and you can and what I won't and I can't. We'll see about this great love of your life. What's his name, by the way? Or am I to refer to him throughout as the great love of your life?"

"Derek O'Teague," I said.

"Stage Irish," said Gordon.

"Why shouldn't it be real Irish?" I asked petulantly.

"Why should he be real anything?" said Gordon. "You yourself had your doubts when you met him."

"I suppose he is Irish," I said.

"Rubbish," said Gordon; "he is as Irish as all those real Irish songs about my little old mother in Ireland, which are thrown together by Polish Jews from Krakow. Go and make loo-loo now. I've had enough of it. We'll go out now."

We walked up Portman Square and into Baker Street to the bus stop. I was glad I had got off the settee and was out and away, in the open air.

I said to myself, I suppose it had to come out sooner or later. And he didn't even say I mustn't see him again.

Gordon, after having said that we would be going to Shepherds, had been silent during our walk, with his head lowered and his eyes on the ground. Now that we came to a halt, he was still silent, and I began to make some fatuous remarks out of my sense of relief. I had just finished saying, "That's already the third number-two bus going in the other direction in the last five minutes," when he turned to me and said casually, "How many abortions have you had?"

I caught my breath.

"One," I said.

He struck me across the face and said in a very low voice, "Don't lie to me."

"Two," I said.

He said, "That's better. And next time I'll hit harder. Here's our bus."

This had never happened to me before, let alone in the street, in full view of passers-by. I was amazed at my own calmness. I might have easily yelled, wept, made a scene, and the thought of this must have occurred to him, too. Now, seeing how indifferent he had been towards such an eventuality, I said to myself, It's no use, he always wins, and a shiver of delicious satisfaction ran through me.

87

While we were riding along Park Lane, I kept looking out for the stop for Curzon Street, and as we were nearing it, I said, "I think that's where we want to get off."

Gordon turned to me and said in the very loud voice of an irate old general, somewhat hard of hearing: "So it is, so it is. Do you have to tell me? Do you think I'm blind, or what? If you saw it, I saw it. Can't you ever hold your tongue and stop babbling, woman?"

By the time we had made our way to the front of the bus, all the passengers were following us with their eyes, some smirking, some with frozen looks. I was hot with embarrassment and laughing against my will. His sense of humour affected me as did everything else about him; it humiliated me, and at the same time I enjoyed it.

Shepherds was crowded and we did not stay long. When we left, he stopped with me in front of the antique shop on the other side of the street and said, "The old and the beautiful. We've come back to it again, haven't we?"

"Naturally," I said, "I don't think the shop will move, any more than Shepherds will."

"Don't keep sidetracking me," he said. "I meant this great love of your life. He's old and he is beautiful, isn't he? But your love for old age must have deeper sources, don't you think?"

"I've never thought about it."

"We'll see, anyway," he said. "I'm going to dissolve him for you," and when I looked at him, bewildered and incredulous, he repeated in a flippant tone of voice, "Oh, yes, I'm going to dissolve him."

While I, falling back on my formula of being afraid, grew impertinent and taunting in order to overcome my uneasiness. I said, "Anyway, it's frightfully lucky for you I'm as well behaved as I am. I could have made a ghastly show-down in Baker Street. I could have screamed the place down."

"Why didn't you?" he asked.

"Because I'm well brought up," I said. "When I was small and yelled or wept, I got my face slapped, to give me something to cry about."

"Just what I thought," he remarked; "but when you were small, and another child hit you, you hit back, didn't you?"

"Of course I did," I said.

"You are a sheer joy," said Gordon.

Chapter

Seven

During that night, after I had first told him about Derek O'Teague, Gordon grabbed me by the hair, jerked my head up, and I awoke from the pain. The bedside lamp was burning.

"You are not to go to sleep on me," said Gordon; "you are here for my amusement. Talk."

I sat up and he said, "Just talk. Anything that comes to your mind."

And when I looked at him, puzzled, he gave another painful tug at my hair: "Go on, talk."

And so I talked, at random, while he lay with his eyes closed and I could not tell whether he was listening or not; but whenever I ceased, saying, "My mind is a complete blank now," he said, "Let your mind roam. Just go on. Talk fifteen to a dozen."

It was perhaps twenty minutes later when he said, "That's enough. Now go back to sleep."

As time went on, I became used to this bizarre procedure, which happened about once every week. Sometimes, I recalled incidents which were well-rounded, proper stories, but mostly I jumped from one thought to another. At first it seemed to me like accompanying the course of the Meander through Phrygia, twisting, turning, forever changing; but it was not like that at all, I soon realised, because after a while the pattern of this river becomes predictable, whereas in my own thoughts I could find no pattern at all. Gordon never interrupted me or questioned me during this, and when I protested that it was "sheer drivel," he would say, "Only to you, my poor child. Not to me. Go on. Talk."

During these nightly talks, though, I enjoyed a complete freedom of movement. I could drape myself over his body any way I liked, or I made him raise his knees and use his sloping legs as a surface to rest my breasts or shoulders on. He was extremely long-suffering on these occasions. He never complained that I weighed too heavily on him or that I dug my chin too sharply into his chest.

That afternoon when I told Gordon my dream of the Belgrave Park Hotel, I did not think he would find out straightaway the nature of my feelings for Derek O'Teague. But even when he did find out at once, and I imagined he might forbid me to see Derek again, it never occurred to me that Gordon might be disgusted with me and might want to stop seeing me; this was because, from other experiences, I knew that Gordon was a man whom "nothing could put off."

For instance, the fourth time I went out with him, we had dinner in a French restaurant in Old Compton Street, and then went back to Portman Square. A few steps before reaching his front door, I tossed my head and said what I had been saving up during the whole evening, "I'll come in and talk, if you want to. But that's all, because I've got the curse."

What I said was true, but I was triumphant about it because I was certain of his disappointment.

To me the monthly bleeding made a woman untouchable beyond question; there is a majesty that clings to it which is even revealed in the slangy term of "curse," a word reverberating with a fear- and awe-inspiring echo resounding from the depths of time.

During my marriage and the year I had lived with Reggie Starr, this period had made me exempt from any amorous contact, and my women friends had taught me how to use the pretext of suffering from menstruation as the easiest way of "putting off" a man.

My triumph was dashed to the ground as soon as it had taken wing.

"Oh, I like women with the curse," said Gordon.

I stopped, incredulous, glancing at his sombre profile.

"Come on, don't dawdle," he said without slowing down his pace.

"You mean you will?" I asked, catching up with him.

"I do," he said.

"But it's impossible," I exclaimed. "For one thing, for the woman. And for the man, too."

"Why?" he asked, fitting his key into the lock.

"I'll bleed to death," I said, improvising on the spur of the moment.

"I'll risk it," he said.

"And I'll get blood poisoning," I added, "because I'm all open and raw inside." This, too, I invented. Like all my girl-friends, I had always taken it for granted that it "couldn't be done," without knowing why.

Gordon remarked, "Once you are dead you won't worry about septicaemia. And what is in store for me? I can hardly wait."

"It's nothing to joke about," I said. "A girl once told me positively that when a man does it when the woman is in that state, he gets a terrible inflammation."

"It does not affect me like that," he remarked, "so you are out of luck, my poor child, with your myths and legends. If at least they were original."

When I lay down on the bed, I was still uneasy and suspicious. He came over to me, stopped, shuddered, groaned, and hid his face in his hands. "You make me feel so guilty," he said, "you've no idea. You don't know what you are doing to me." He watched me as I laughed. Then he said, "I'll teach you something new. Do you know what the Gorgo Medusa is?"

"Of course," I said.

"But do you know what it means?" he asked. "The horrible face surrounded by coils of snakes?—one look at it and you get turned to stone?"

I shook my head.

"Open your legs," he said, and when I did so, he added, "It's this. What you are showing me."

"You mean——?" I asked.

"Yes," he said; "no eye must ever behold it. And now you made me look at it. Oh, how could you be so cruel?" and he gave another exaggerated shudder. I stopped laughing when he took possession of me.

But though he had overcome within a few minutes my life-long belief about the sacredness of the monthly bleeding, he never conquered my feelings about the face of the Gorgo Medusa. For instance, often, while possessing me, he raised his body away from mine and watched himself in the act of using me, and this always made me feel that he was infringing against a law.

As I have said, with Gordon I always slept "fast," sunk into uninterrupted profound darkness, without the usual intervals of half-dreamy, half-conscious states which make one aware, by rising and again submerging into the depths, that one is sleeping.

Yet on one occasion I came to, during the night, not certain whether I was asleep or awake. The bedside lamp was burning. I found that I was lying on my back with the covers stripped off me, and I saw Gordon kneeling at the foot of the bed, with his head bent over my parted thighs. His countenance, as far as I could see it, wore a look of intense concentration, and I felt his hand folding back my lips and turning them over, as though he were leafing through the pages of a book, searching to find an important quotation in the text.

"What on earth are you doing?" I asked.

"Keep still," he said. "I'm looking at you. I want to see if you are sexually pretty. You are. You are the only woman I've ever come across who is actually sexually pretty."

I was hot and flushed with shame and at the same time I was glad that he was able to make me feel so ashamed.

"Stop it; this is ridiculous," I cried.

"Be quiet," he said, continuing to leaf through me with grave concentration.

Nobody had ever looked at those parts of me, and the very idea as to their possible "prettiness" had never occurred to me; I did not even know what they looked like myself.

"It's all wrong. Leave me alone!" I cried, tossing about.

He put his hands round my hips and gripped me tight.

"Go back to sleep," he said.

"I can't sleep on my back," I said.

"Of course you can," he remarked, without raising his head. "You are so tired, my poor child, you can't even keep your eyes open. You are so deeply tired, you are just sinking into deep sleep, you are sinking deeper down into sleep, all the time."

I cannot remember whether I kept on with my protests, nor can I remember whether I really went to sleep lying on my back. The next thing I knew was that I awoke in full daylight and found him dressed and beautifully groomed, as usual, sitting by my bedside, and watching me.

I had, after this, the absurd conviction that he kept exploring me from time to time without my knowing it; and when I recall his voice and his words on that night, I feel, even now, so tired and heavy-lidded, that if I gave way and lay down, I would fall asleep.

Chapter

Eight

Reggie Starr once said to me about Jessie Ryan, the continuity girl, "I do my homework. She comes. Then she can go on with her knitting."

With me and Gordon it was never like this. He never went back to his knitting. When he was with me, he gave me his full attention all the time. That his attention was often painful was true. I had to submit to it and he gave me no choice. But even if I had had the choice, I would have preferred it this way; it is better to be punished than not to be punished, because not to get punished means being treated with indifference. There are no spectacular sunsets without a clouded sky.

Thus, when Gordon stopped the talks about "my long hair" and replaced them instead with talks about the Belgrave Park Hotel, I was gratified by this proof of his interest in me, though I kept putting obstacles in his path, just as I used to clench my legs when he wanted to take possession of me; and being forced to give satisfactory replies was similar to having to give way to his virility.

The Belgrave Park Hotel was to me a monument of dishonesty, deceit, and betrayal, because it was there that I had stayed for a few days, in the fifth year of my marriage, on the pretext of coming to London to see my cousin Sylvia. My plan had been to find myself some work and then to leave my husband.

It was two days before I was due to return to Leicester that I met Derek O'Teague, in a tea-shop in Piccadilly. The waitress led me to the table where he was sitting, asking me whether I wouldn't "mind joining the gentleman," and as she pulled out the chair for me, he half rose from his seat.

I cast my eyes down at the table littered with the remnants of his tea, buttered toast and honey, and at the opened gold case in which black gold-tipped cigarettes reposed like the keys of an exotic miniature harpsichord.

"Would you care for one of my cigarettes?" he asked.

"Yes," I said, "they look fascinating. I've never seen such cigarettes before."

"I have them made for me," he remarked.

I thought, Oh, God, I have them made for me, which was, no doubt, exactly what he wanted me to think.

"Here comes the old trout," he said, bending towards me with his gold lighter. "Don't take any muffins or buns. They're like leather. Order toast. It's the only thing fit to eat in this place."

"All right," I said, laughing. "I had no idea. I haven't been here since the war started. Do you come here often?"

"Sometimes," he said. "I go everywhere. Rising to heights and sinking to depths. I have to."

"Why?" I asked.

He let his eyes roam over the place before replying. "I am all sorts of things," he said, "and among others, I'm an author."

Like Hell, I thought. I had never met an author before, but I had noticed the pause and the hesitation. I said, pointedly, "In that case, I suppose, you have to put your feelings and your ecstasies on ice."

"Oh, you've read *Tonio Kroeger*," he said.

I blushed. I had not expected this.

After we left Logan's, we walked through Green Park and sat on a bench. It was a mild grey day in March and the air was heavy and still.

He told me he had been in the army for two years, had taken part in the Norway campaign, and was now out of it for good. "I laughed and I cried," he said, "and I put a revolver to my head. My batman reported me. These psychiatrists, you can tell them anything. So here I am, thank God." It was an ambiguous way of telling his story and I thought that, considering that people were still quarrelling over Hamlet's real or pretended madness, it was not for me to try and sort it out. "Anyway, I was too old for the army," he remarked; "yes, I am very old. How old are you?"

"Twenty-four," I said.

"Oh, in the presence of twenty-four, and such charming twenty-four, people like me shouldn't be allowed to breathe," he said.

"Oh, stop pulling my leg," I said. "You can't be over thirty."

"Can't I?" he said. "Do you know, at the last medical in the army, the doctor patted me on the shoulder and said, 'All right, my lad,' and I said to him, 'Young man, you were still in your pram when I was having drinks in the green plush and gold of the Café Royal.' Of course you don't know the Café Royal, my dear, as it was in the old days. It's red velvet now."

"Oh, come off it," I said.

"But it's true," he remarked. "I am one of the ancients. I know what I am and where I'm going. Not like you people. You will be somewhere, my dear, one day, with your lovely dark crisp hair white and thin, and I'll be still walking about just the way I am now," and when I kept silent, he added, "You don't believe me. You think it can't be done."

"No. I think it can't be done," I said.

"Why not?" he asked, twisting his gold-topped cane which,

like his gold watch, gold lighter, and gold case, pin-pointed the magnificence of his appearance.

"I'm not saying you can't live long," I said; "say, you can live for ninety years. But people who want to live long always make one mistake. They forget that if they have a long life they have to grow very old. If you see what I mean."

"Exactly," he said; "if people live long they have to grow old. That's where your mistake lies. You've seen only the way old people look. But I say I can live very long and stay young."

"But you can't," I exclaimed; "nobody can."

"You mean you've seen nobody who could. Is that right?" he said.

"Yes," I said.

"And because you've seen nobody who could, you say it can't be done. Correct?" he asked.

"Yes," I said.

"And you are wrong," he remarked. "Let us suppose you have never been to Spain. Are you going to say that Spain does not exist?"

"Of course not," I said.

"There you are," he said. "Because you don't know something and you've never seen it, it doesn't mean it isn't true, my dear," and when I glanced at him from beneath lowered lashes, thinking, What do I care? He's marvellous to look at, anyway, he added, "Now you can't make up your mind whether I'm serious or not. I'm not, of course. I was only joking. I was only trying to see how long you'd stay your ground." And as I was still gazing at him, he said, "You are very firmly planted on the ground, though, with your little feet. What a lovely little foot you've got, by the way—or is that an irrelevant thing to say?"

He saw me back to my hotel and asked if he could come round

and take me out to dinner in the evening. We went to a Chinese restaurant in Shaftesbury Avenue.

"And what did he treat you with, at dinner?" asked Gordon at this point in my story.

"A clear soup with green and grey strands floating in it," I said. "It made me think of mermaid's hair. It had a melancholy flavour, too, like the Andersen fairy-tale."

"Don't side-track me," said Gordon. "You know quite well what I mean. Come off the poetic soup. What did he give you in the way of patter?"

"Reincarnation," I said. "He'd been here before and he'd come back again, and when I said he couldn't prove it, he said he couldn't prove it but I couldn't disprove it either."

Gordon said, "And then he started talking about scientists and doctors, and how stupid they are, and how they don't know anything worth knowing."

"How do you know?" I exclaimed. "You weren't there."

"Wasn't I?" said Gordon. "And then, he hinted he had magic powers. What magic powers?"

I said, "If he didn't want to, he didn't cast a reflection in the mirror. And he would show me one day."

"I've seen it done, too," said Gordon. "I've known people who didn't cast their reflection in the mirror. Everybody saw their reflection, only they didn't. And I've seen those people who have eternal youth and beauty, too. Every loony-bin is full of them, my poor child."

"But he never said it outright," I remarked, "or, when he said it, he took it back again and said he was talking symbolically."

"Just trying it on," said Gordon; "in that state they know quite well with whom they can and with whom they can't. What does he talk like, when you see him now?"

"He talks film gossip, like everybody else at Delmain's—

that's the coffee shop where I always meet him. He's always with film people."

"And when he is alone with you?" asked Gordon.

"He gets on to the magic stuff," I said, "but I can't really tell if he believes it."

"Oh yes, he does," said Gordon.

"But he can't be mad," I said. "He'll be doing the lead in a film now. It's only held up because the producer—anyway, he's a very competent actor, they say. But he's not an author, really; that was rot he told me. Because he's only written this one book of measly memoirs."

"These people can lead very successful lives," said Gordon. "He's not what you'd call mad in the way that he's got to be locked up. But, medically speaking, he is mad, of course. But that's the least of it. It's all so boring. I know it all by heart."

"Well, to me it wasn't boring," I said, "and I didn't know it all by heart. And he was so beautiful I couldn't take my eyes off him. So it didn't really matter to me if it was all rot or not. And I kept wondering about his being an author, because when I asked him about his writing, he said it was queer stuff and left it at that."

"And did you think you were in love with him then?" asked Gordon.

"No," I said, "that's the funny part about it. It was just that he was something so out of the ordinary for me—what with being married in Leicester—and never meeting anybody but engineers, and talk of fishing and shooting and racing cars—can't you understand?"

"And what happened then?" asked Gordon.

I said, "I saw him the next day again, for tea and dinner. And he gave me his name. But not his address. I gave him mine, though. And he said he'd write to me. And then I went back to

Leicester and he never wrote. And I had nothing but his name and I thought even that was made up."

"So you doubted everything about him from the beginning," said Gordon. "That's very interesting."

"And yet, I mean, it wasn't fair of me," I said. "For instance, the way he placed that phrase out of *Tonio Kroeger* straightaway. He did know his Thomas Mann. It's more than you know. But even so—I don't know—"

"Even so, you didn't swallow his line," said Gordon; "and yet, later on—but we'll see."

That evening when Gordon told me to undress and lie down, I did undress, but instead of lying down I remained standing in front of the bed. I was in a particularly rebellious mood, owing to our talk in the afternoon, and when he came towards me I said, "I'm sick and tired of this love-making of yours. Always the same, always bread-and-butter, and nothing else ever occurs to you."

"Lie down," he said, unmoved.

I lay down and spread my thighs apart the way he wanted it. It was true, of course, that he never took me in any other position, but what I had said was not true. I did want to be on my back, with him above me, and if he had used me in any other way I would not have liked it, because I would not have had the feeling of being helplessly dominated.

I gasped as he entered my body slowly and deliberately, and then went on with a fierceness which made me sigh and tremble with delight, as each time he withdrew to the very edge and returned to invade me more deeply. I trembled with longing to receive him as he withdrew once more; and then gave a stifled shriek.

He had not returned to me. He had done what Goethe expressed with such heartless elegance in his distich:

Knaben habe ich gern, doch habe ich lieber die Mädchen.
Ist sie als Mädchen mir satt, brauch ich als Knabe sie noch.

That is,

> I like boys, but I do prefer girls.
> Once I've had enough of her as a girl,
> I can still make use of her as a boy.

At his first painful stab of using me as a boy, I was filled, apart from my revulsion, with incredulity, imagining that he had done it by mistake. But while he, as though unaware of my distress, forced himself in further, with an irrevocable determination, I started to scream: "No, don't! You're not to!"

I tried to claw at him with my nails, but he was far away from me, with his arms and body well out of my reach. I still could not believe that he was really doing this to me, this revolting indecency, all the more so as I had always imagined that this kind of contact could only be achieved when the passive partner was kneeling down. If anyone had been observing us it would have looked like ordinary love-making, and I fiercely resented it that he had managed to inflict this outrage on me by practising a kind of deceit.

As he pressed down inside me and widened me with each new stab, the disgusting pain gave way to a dull discomfort, which dwindled into a vague unease and then ceased all together.

I was now completely and comfortably open to him, and this, the fact that my body had stopped resisting and had thus betrayed me, made me burst into new protests. He went on for a long time, with his usual grim thoroughness.

When he left me, I rolled over, buried my face in the crook of my folded arms, and gave way to my tears. I did not weep the violent spasmodic tears of rage with their jerking sobs, but the gently flowing tears of despair. From time to time as I grabbed hold of the corner of the sheet to dry my face, I saw him sitting on the edge of the bed, observing me; during all this time he neither spoke one word of consolation, nor did he touch me with a reassuring hand, nor did he give me a handkerchief. I was beyond such trivialities as handkerchiefs, though. It was only later, when I marshalled my grievances against him, that this came to my mind.

I went on weeping, feeling deserted and alone. My tears flowed in the way it rains; I did not weep, it wept me. And when I stopped, it was again beyond my control. I had run dry.

"You have been weeping for exactly one hour," he said.

I remained silent.

He added, "You've been carrying on as though you'd been raped."

"It was like that, too," I said. "It's never happened to me before."

"I've never done it before, either," he said.

"Why did you do it?" I asked.

"Because I was annoyed with you," he said, "when you made the remark about my love-making always being the same. But you'll bite your teeth out on me, my poor child, I promise you."

I hid my face again.

I was glad that I had been able to offend him after all. But beyond this satisfaction there flowed the much deeper, familiar, truly fulfilling gratification of my being—that he had punished me and given me a much greater distress than I had given him.

This was the only time he ever made me weep. What he did to me later on was beyond tears. He never again used me like a boy and neither of us ever mentioned it again. He took me once more that night and made me laugh by saying, "Oh, what couldn't I do to a nice woman. Oh, if only I were in bed with a nice woman now."

When Gordon took me home on the following morning, he said: "I shan't see you tonight. I'm going out with a friend of mine. Bruce. He's in the papers just now; he's giving psychiatric evidence at the Heath trials."

"Oh, really," I said; "I wouldn't know. I never read the papers. I got fed up with them for good during the war. The only thing which interests me is when the rationing is going to be over. And if my grocer doesn't know it, it's not worth knowing."

"Bruce is a nice man," said Gordon. "The only trouble with him is, he likes morphine."

"Oh, how ghastly," I exclaimed.

"Don't talk rubbish," said Gordon; "it's not ghastly. It's just that I don't care for it myself. Sometimes when we get together I take half a grain to keep him company. But it doesn't do anything to me. I take heroin."

"No, you are joking," I said; "it's not true."

"Oh, yes, I take heroin," he said with the same slow emphasis as when he had told me about having had syphilis; and then, while I was still looking at him, hoping that the horror I felt did not show too much, he gave one of his scathing grins and said, "Strictly not habit-forming, of course," in the same falsely jovial voice he used when telling me: "Lie down on the bed. No sex and no cruelty, of course."

"Well," I said, giving him a resigned glance.

"I shan't take you along, my poor child," he said, "because if Bruce saw you, he'd be absolutely delighted with you. I must take good care you never meet him."

Chapter

Nine

W hen I went to see Gordon two days later, he told me as
soon as I entered, "I've had a girl here, last night."

"Did you?" I said, following him into the room. My heart did
not beat with anxiety, nor did it shrivel with fear, nor did it swell
with bitterness.

"Yes," he said, watching me with a smile, "and she was most
enthusiastic. She said she wanted to come again."

"Oh, really?" I said, laughing. "And when will she come?"

"She won't," he said.

"Why not?" I asked.

"Because it's no good," he said. "I'm too much involved
with you," and he turned his back on me and walked over to the
window.

I thought: Involved. Why can't he use decent English? Why
must he hide behind his jargon? Why can't he say he loves me?

I said, "But what if—wouldn't it help?" I said it with friendly
concern. It was genuine, and I could afford it. I felt as safe and
serene as two days before, when he had told me that he would see
to it that I would never meet Bruce.

"No, it wouldn't help," he said, moving away from the window and towards the desk, with his eyes cast down: "It wouldn't
help. When it's like this nothing helps. And you know it as well
as I do."

He opened a drawer in his desk. "Sit down now. And go on

from where you left off. The great love of your life. So he didn't write to you and you never heard from him again."

"Yes," I said, "and I was cross. Because he'd kept telling me during those two days in London that I was lovely."

"What? Lovely?" said Gordon with a sardonic smile.

"Yes," I said, tossing my head.

"You—lovely?" said Gordon with a laugh of false joviality. "My poor child! He was pulling your leg."

"Oh, leave me alone," I said haughtily.

But I did gain a triumph a few days later, when Gordon paid me a compliment, after all, though it was oblique and cross-grained.

It was on one of those occasions when I refused to undress, and he said, "Get it off before I tear it off," and while he was watching me undress, he remarked, "Every time I see you getting out of these corsets it makes my blood boil."

"Why?" I asked, greatly astonished.

He was the only man I had ever known who was free from the tiresome habit of remarking, "Now, why don't you wear—" or, "You'd look marvellous if you'd put on—" and I was therefore astonished that he was finding fault with this under-garment.

"And, anyway," I said cheekily, "what are you complaining about? It isn't as though you have to undress me. I'm doing it all by myself."

I was very fond of these corsets. They were of thin sky-blue cotton, with the hallmarks of expensive workmanship, such as a lining of pale blue velvet under the shoulder-straps and a strip of the same velvet beneath the zip-fastener, so as to avoid pressure marks on the skin. "It was made specially for me, to measure," I added.

"Don't say 'specially,' say 'especially,' " said Gordon.

"Yes," I said, "but what's wrong with them?"

"They make my blood boil," he said, "because you don't need

to wear them, with that body of yours," and he added with a voice tightened with rage, "You should not wear anything at all."

He had never before given me the least cause to suspect that he was aware of the loveliness of my body, all the more so as he never touched me in a caress, and I kept wearing the sky-blue corsets as a gesture of defiance. When I stopped seeing Gordon, I gave them to the charwoman to use as a floorcloth. I have never worn corsets since.

"So you were cross when he didn't write to you," said Gordon now, "and by the way, it has just occurred to me that he is a fake, even about his famous age. If he was in the army—and that sounds true—invalided out with a breakdown—he can't have been as old as he gave you to understand. His age was put on to impress you with his magic powers. So, what it boils down to is, he's about forty, and looks it. But the age you swallowed, didn't you?"

"Yes," I said, "the green decor in the Café Royal sounded so convincing, for instance. And he never gave me any dates. I couldn't pin him down. Anyway, as time went on, I got more than cross. I kept puzzling over what he really was and who he really was, and I wanted to find him again. 'Time the great healer' is all rot, you know. It's like being thirsty. The longer you wait, the thirstier you get, and if you have something that worries you it gets worse all the time."

"It was not worry," said Gordon; "you worry about something reasonable, like how to find the money for next month's rent. But with you it wasn't the rent. It was you against yourself. It was like something eating inside you, a little mouse in your heart, fretting all the time, wasn't it?"

"Yes," I said, "and then the WRENS wrote to say they'd like to have me, and I wrote back and turned them down because it was a job where I wouldn't have been an officer. But this wasn't why I turned them down; I'd known that already when I had my interview with them in London, that time. It was because the WRENS would have sent me God knows where, and that didn't suit me, I wanted to get to London to find out about him and to meet him again. I didn't mind what I did as long as I could get back to London. I couldn't think about anything else any more. I know it sounds idiotic."

Gordon said, "It sounds like the obsessions people had in the Middle Ages, when they said they were bewitched and under a spell. No, don't laugh, I mean it seriously. That was how it felt, wasn't it?"

"Yes," I said; "and then I got taken on by the American War Department, through a girl-friend of mine who worked in one of their branches in Leicester, and they were all moving to London just then, and I discarded my husband and gave him all the jam I'd made, because he said it belonged to him, and sold all the stuff that belonged to me. I got a lot for the Persian carpets and the china and the linen, some of it still from my great-grandmother's which had never been used—all Irish linen—and I only kept a few small things like a napkin from the court of the Emperor Franz-Josef, and I went to London with the Americans. They were nice and easygoing, and I could be as lazy as I wanted to; they couldn't throw anybody out, because they'd have got into trouble with the Labour Exchange. And there were parties going on all the time, and there was the good American food we got from their mess, and everything would have been fine if it hadn't been for this. I just didn't know where to start looking for him. Then I met Reggie Starr, the film director, and got in with his crowd, and there were writers among them, too. I asked them all about Derek O'Teague, the author, and nothing ever came of it. They usually said, yes, the name was somehow—and then, perhaps, it wasn't. By then I was quite desperate. Till my cousin Sylvia came along. She is very brainy, and besides, she got fed up with my nagging and whining. So one day, when I was again moaning to her, during the lunch hour, when we used to meet, she took me to Wigmore Street to the Times Bookshop and we walked in and she said to the assistant, 'I want a book by Derek O'Teague, but I've forgotten the publisher and the title. Will you look it up for me?' and the assistant came back and said there was only one book by that author, anyhow, and they didn't have it in stock but they could order it. It took my breath away. And I ordered it. It really existed. He really existed. What do you say now?"

"I'll say it later," said Gordon. "Go on."

"When I got the book, I opened it. And there on the title page was his photograph—so it was really him—and it was some kind of reminiscences, called *The Abyss of Time,* all itsy-bitsies chopped up, trying to be like Oscar Wilde's epigrams. And then—nothing again. Because when I thought I'd write to him in care of the publishers, it turned out they didn't exist any more. Folded up in the beginning of the war. I felt like howling."

"Very nice," said Gordon, "the quest for the mysterious, evasive man. Chasing the unknown."

"I still didn't give up," I said. "I went with the British to Germany, because they gave me much better pay and made me a captain. And in the messes I started asking round the likely officers—the ones that had been in the Norway campaign—and one of them knew him. He'd run into him in London, while on leave, and was shocked because he wore make-up, but beyond this he couldn't say, either. And so it went on. And it didn't stop. Then I went to London on leave and I met my cousin Sylvia in our café on the corner of Dean Street. It was so full we couldn't get a table. Sylvia said, 'There's another café round the corner which is also ever so atmospheric, we'll go there, it's Delmain's in Rupert Street.' And when we get through the door, there he is, the gold-topped cane leaning against his chair and the black-and-gold cigarettes on the table and a crowd of men sitting round him. I told Sylvia, 'He's here, please go to Hell, do you mind?' And she went, she's incredibly decent."

"And then you went to bed with him straightaway," said Gordon. "You couldn't wait, could you? You were burning by then."

"Yes," I said, "I took him to my place—I mean, it was Reggie's place in Sloane Square—I was spending my leave there, with him. I knew Reggie would be out shooting on location and wouldn't be there, but even if he had come home, I wouldn't have cared. I didn't care about anything. When Reggie came home in the evening, I told him I had found the man I had always wanted."

"That's not quite true," said Gordon. "You thought you had found the man you had always wanted. But it wasn't. Never mind. Don't worry your pretty little head about it now, my angel."

"That's so exactly like you," I said; "up you come with your piece of wisdom and one thinks it's something, and then it doesn't add up to anything."

"And Reggie the Filmmaker didn't cut up rough?" asked Gordon.

"No, not he," I said. "He just took it."

"Very stupid of him," said Gordon. "I suppose he didn't know any better."

"Reggie's weak," I said; "charming, but soft and floppy like a bedroom slipper. And then I went back to Germany and handed in my resignation. They wanted me to stay on. Colonel Prior talked to me like a sick horse; even the brigadier saw me and drivelled how they'd miss having me round—but there was no holding me. I served till the end of my year and then I chucked it. But don't you think it's extraordinary how I found him, after all those years? It took me three years to walk from Logan's in Piccadilly to Delmain's in Rupert Street."

"There is only one thing which is remarkable about the story," said Gordon, "and that has never occurred to you. Why did you not want to go to bed with him in the first place? His looks hadn't changed, had they? Or did he wear better make-up when you saw him three years later?"

"Oh, leave him alone," I said.

"I'll leave him alone," said Gordon; "he doesn't interest me. My only interest is in the three years' interval, when you did not see him. We can start getting back to your dream now."

"But I've told you my dream already," I said.

"Yes," said Gordon, "but it will keep me happy for weeks. Don't you think I'm very easy to keep happy?"

"Yes," I said; "and this reminds me of what young Dent told me when he came to our mess. Before he got posted with us, in Hamburg, he was with another outfit in India, and he got fed up and went to the army psychiatrist. He said it was simply Heaven, psychiatrists are so easy to make happy, you just unload all your filth on them and they are so touchingly grateful for it. And after Dent had made him happy, the psychiatrist wrote a letter saying that Dent must get back to Europe because he was suffering from a tropical neurosis, and when Dent asked him what it was, the doctor said he didn't know himself. But then, I'm not young Dent, and I've got no filth to unload."

"No, my sweet child," said Gordon, "we'll keep it strictly clean. Nothing that would not be fit for little children, I promise you," and he gave a horribly cheerful grin.

Chapter

Ten

That evening Gordon said he would take me with him to dinner at a friend of his, a colleague, who was a commisioner of lunacy. "His wife is a doctor, too," he said.

"I shan't open my mouth," I said; "she must be terribly brainy."

"No," he said, "just a stupid woman."

They lived in South Kensington, off the Cromwell Road, in a tall, dark-red-brick house with Dutch scrolled gables and tiny coloured-glass windows flanking the entrance door. The inside looked not only shabby; it looked improvised, as though its inhabitants had either just moved in, or were on the point of moving out, lacking proper furniture and carrying on as best they could.

There were crates with scraps of cloth flung over them serving as occasional tables; kitchen chairs, folding canvas chairs, and wooden slatted garden chairs for seats; cardboard boxes were stacked with books and papers; and kitchen pails did duty as waste-paper baskets. In the living room was a standard lamp of which the cord crept across the floor and was connected to a plug in the hall, which prevented the door from ever being shut.

The commissioner and his wife were both in their forties, quiet, friendly, plump and round-faced; he bald and with glasses, she with greying brown hair swept up untidily into curls on top of her head. He was in old tweeds and flannels. She wore a checked cotton housecoat and sandals.

"We'll have dinner in half an hour's time," she told us. "We are also having my husband's sister," and, lowering her voice to a whisper: "You must be very careful what you say to her. She's got a mother-fixation."

"What's that?" I asked.

She opened her eyes wide with surprise: "Don't you know?" and turning to Gordon: "You said this was your girl-friend. Don't you ever talk to her?"

"Don't start putting ideas into her head," said Gordon. "Talk to her? What next?"

I offered to help her get the meal ready. I hate helping women in their kitchens, just as I loathe it when a woman guest comes to help me in mine. It is only with people like my cousin Sylvia that I don't mind it, and in that case it is not done to help or be helped but to enable us to carry on with our talk.

I followed her into the scullery where, as I had expected, I did nothing but stand about.

The main dish was sausage meat in a casserole, covered with mashed potatoes and browned in the oven; it was put on the table set in the adjoining kitchen. There was plenty of bread and margarine, a slab of cake, the anonymous non-committal cheese which was part of the rations, and many half-empty jars with chutneys and pickles.

There I found, already seated, together with the two men, the sister with the mother-fixation, and the twins belonging to the couple, a boy and a girl of five, with large round heads and shovel ears, identically dressed in smocks and trousers.

The sister was a buxom young woman with red cheeks and frizzy brown hair; she looked patient and kind-hearted, and I felt sure that if I, say, had been knitting or typewriting, she would have picked up my fallen stitches or changed the ribbon on my machine. She kept quiet, as did I.

Later on, when she did join in the talk, it was always to remark something like, "That's exactly the way mother feels, too," or, "Mother wouldn't have touched him with a barge pole, she knew straightaway, she always can tell," and I concluded from this that a mother-fixation was the name for loving and respecting one's mother, just as the expression "to be involved" meant to be in love.

I had been placed next to Gordon, and from time to time I looked at him sideways. He never looked at me, and ignored me.

After dinner the twins were put to bed by their mother, while we remained at the oilcloth-covered table over the luke-warm coffee. Gordon talked to his friend about the decision of a board. I hardly listened.

The wife returned and began to question Gordon over the emotional welfare of the twins. They were sharing a bedroom. Was it wise? Should she not, now that they would be going to school soon, put them in separate rooms? After all, it wasn't as though they were both of the same sex.

"Whatever you do, it's too late now," said Gordon. "They are five. They've had it."

"Oh, don't say that," she wailed. "And what about the Oedipus complex? They've never been to a kindergarten. I had them hanging around me all the time. Was that wrong?"

"That's all done and finished with, too," said Gordon.

"Then there is nothing I can do about it any more?" she asked.

In the course of the meal she had also let fall such expressions as "to identify with," in connection with her charwoman. This person, it appeared, "identified herself with" one of her employers, which was lucky, because she kept the house beautifully clean, but unlucky because she was impertinent to her employer's husband, who was on bad terms with his wife. From this I gathered that "to identify with" someone meant again to like, and to be fond of.

Now, when I heard the question about the Oedipus complex, I knew vaguely what it meant, as vaguely as did most of my friends and acquaintances. Gordon had never mentioned it. I had never given it any thought; I accepted it the way I accepted that the earth was round and turned round the sun, which meant that I did not know about it from my own experience, and neither cared nor was curious to verify the truth of it.

I got suddenly annoyed by the use of all this jargon. Perhaps I was "identifying with" the sister, feeling that my hosts were jeering at her because of an emotion that was perfectly nice and laudable.

I said, "I'll tell you about your twins and their Oedipus complex. In the morning they walk on four legs, at mid-day on two legs and in the evening on three legs, and they'll do this like everybody else."

The wife stared at me and said, "What do you mean?"

I said, "This was the riddle the Sphinx asked him when he came to the gates of Thebes."

"Who?" she asked.

"Oedipus," I said, "the gent you were talking about."

"That's a new one to me," she remarked.

"It's not as new as all that," I said.

"I'd no idea," she said.

"The Sphinx was staggered, too," I said, "when he solved the riddle."

"But that has nothing to do with the Oedipus complex," she said.

"Of course it has," I said. "How can you use the term if you don't even know the story behind it?"

"My wife isn't a psychiatrist," said the commissioner, "and even many psychiatrists don't know the riddle of the Sphinx."

"Then they are like plumbers," I said.

The commissioner turned to Gordon: "You should tell this to Crombie," he said. "Crombie would love it. Do you know his latest? He wants everybody who gets training to be familiar with the masterpieces of literature."

"I think your girl-friend is amazing," said the wife; "such a little girl, when I first saw her I thought butter couldn't melt in her mouth. But she's got her opinions. How did you first get to know her?"

"On a bench in a garden," said Gordon; "but she didn't have any opinions then."

I felt he was watching me. I turned my face away.

I kept silent for the rest of the evening and spent the time imagining what a dinner at Crombie's would be like. The dining room was large, with a stucco-work ceiling, and furnished with imitation Chippendale. The dinner was composed of at least four courses. Dr. Crombie insisted on these despite the difficulties of rationing; they were conventional and badly cooked. Sardines on toast, clear soup, with perhaps an Australian sherry, roast leg of lamb with sprouts and chipped potatoes, and a Stilton cheese sent by a grateful patient, whom Dr. Crombie had severed from his mother-fixation. Now the patient did not love his mother any more and Crombie had the Stilton.

At eleven o'clock Gordon said to me, "Come, my poor child. We must go. You are so tired, you are quite pale."

The commissioner, who had left the kitchen a few minutes before, returned, saying, "You can't go. There's a bad fog. You'll never get home tonight."

The wife showed me to a room three flights up. I helped her put the sheets on the camp-bed, while making the usual apologies for putting her to so much trouble.

When she left me, and I got into bed and turned the light out, I did not know where Gordon had got to. He had stayed behind when I went upstairs. I stayed awake, listening, hoping he would come. I added butter and biscuits to the Stilton cheese. There was only real butter on Dr. Crombie's table; the whole household, including the maid with scabies, saved up their butter ration, because Crombie, with integrity and intransigence, did not tolerate margarine on the lace-covered board of gleaming mahogany.

I was wakened in the morning by the little girl, who watched me doing my hair, handed me the pins, and rearranged the contents of my handbag. I met Gordon on the first-floor landing, together with the little boy. Gordon leered at me. "As you see," he said, "there's been a strict division of the sexes, even in the calling service provided," and, glancing at my little companion: "Ah, yes. That's what I really need, a little girl of five. Oh, what couldn't I do with a little girl of five."

We followed the twins into the basement.

The commissioner was at the kitchen table still littered with the pickle jars and bottles of the previous night. He was reading a paper.

The wife, in the same checked housecoat, greeted us with a jolly, knowing smile. I felt her glance travelling over my face, probably looking for dark shadows under my eyes, and I was certain she had sent up the twins in order to find out if Gordon and I had spent the night together.

I was again placed next to Gordon, seated at his left. I declined all food and took nothing but coffee. The wife, after having served Gordon with cereals and sausages, poured herself another cup and took a chair near me, at the head of the table.

"Did you sleep well?" she asked, observing me with a good-natured, expectant, conspiratorial air.

"Yes, thank you," I said, laughing. "The house is marvellously quiet. I slept like a log."

"Oh," she said, and effacing the look of disappointment on her countenance, she added with a hostess's polite cheerfulness, "I'm so glad," giving Gordon a glance of whimsical reproach.

Gordon was eating with his head lowered and without looking up. But he reached out with his left hand and closed it round my wrist just as I was about to get hold of my cup. I caught my breath and placed my hand on the table and kept it there, fettered in his grasp. I raised my cup with my left hand and took a sip of coffee, pretending to listen to what the wife was saying.

Gordon let go of me for a short time while he helped himself to bread and butter and marmalade, and then his hand returned to me and closed round my pulse, with a sudden painful tightening which made me gasp.

At a loss for what to say, I looked at my hostess, and seeing the bangles of beaten silver which I had noticed on her arm the night before, and knowing from experience that it was always safe to admire on people what to me was most conspicuously distasteful, I remarked, "I do like your bracelets. They are something native, aren't they?"

"Yes," she said, looking down at her arm with a pleased smile; "they are from Morocco."

And while I listened to her telling me how and where she had bought them, I wriggled my imprisoned arm, trying to free myself, but was forced at once into submissive stillness as Gordon, without giving me a glance, turned my wrist and sent a flicker of pain through me.

"How can you stand him pawing you like this all the time?" said the wife. "It would drive me crazy."

"He's not pawing me, he's just holding me," I said, falling into her somewhat insulting mode of speech, which dealt with Gordon as though he were a dumb animal whom one could discuss freely.

"Even so. How can you stand it?" she said.

"I don't mind it. I'm used to him," I said.

"He's going to marry you, isn't he?" she asked.

"No," I said.

"I'm sure he'll marry you," she said; "but do you think you could put up with him? Have you thought about it?"

"Never," I said.

"Oh, come on, of course you have," she exclaimed; "you've got your opinions about everything. So you're not going to tell me—"

"No, I haven't, really," I said.

"What a strange little girl you are," she said.

Gordon all the time had continued to eat.

The commissioner, as far as I could see, was still reading the paper. If he was listening at all, I could not tell, but the thought of this eventuality did not distress me. Dealing with lunacy, he was, I felt, used to more peculiar conversations.

As we were emerging into the Cromwell Road, I said to Gordon, "Why didn't you come to my room?"

"Did you mind?" he asked.

"Yes," I said. "I felt like the Emperor Marcus Aurelius, with his *diem perdidi*, I mean, *noctem*, though."

Gordon said, "The Emperor Marcus Aurelius did not have to

worry about noise. I wasn't going to have them listening to your screams, my sweet child."

"Oh," I said, "I hadn't been thinking—"

"I knew you weren't," he said; "you are like a child of five. One has to think of everything for you."

"Yes," I said.

"You can't even understand your own dreams," he said. "One has to tell you every step. But I shan't marry you."

"Oh, God, what on earth—" I exclaimed; "and only because she said—you think you—"

"No," he said. "She's just a stupid woman. But I have been thinking about it, seriously."

I was astonished. "Have you?" I asked.

"Yes, I have."

I had never thought of getting married to him. I had never even had any daydreams about what it might be like. Which, perhaps, was the more strange, as our hostess, the "stupid woman," had hit on the idea straightaway. And why, if I went as far as to see the unknown Dr. Crombie presiding at his dining table, had I stopped short at Gordon, whom I knew so well?

"And I'll tell you why I won't marry you," he said. "Because I know exactly the points over which we would quarrel."

I would have dearly liked to be told what those points were, but did not dare to ask. I never found out. He never spoke of it again.

We continued for a while in silence.

When we got to the bus stop, he said, "Yes, she's just a stupid woman. Do you think, by the way, that women can have the Oedipus complex, too?" and he watched me with that cold fascination.

What's he driving at? I wondered. I said, "Don't be so idiotic. How can a woman marry her mother? Even if she could kill her father."

"She'd just have to do the reverse, my poor child," he said; "she'd have to kill her mother and marry her father."

"Oh, God," I said, flaring up; "you do think of everything. You really are——"

"I am disgusting, I know," he said, "but I didn't invent it. And it's got a name, too. It's called the Elektra complex. Here is our bus."

The bus was almost empty. We walked up to the front and took the foremost seats.

I asked, "But why is she so worried about the twins sleeping together in the same room? What does she expect them to get up to? They are only five. But even if they weren't. Is that another complex she's got on her brain, or what?"

"It's not only in her brain," said Gordon. "Things do happen, you know. I seduced two of my sisters. One was thirteen at the time and the other fourteen."

I felt myself turning pale and fell back on my formula of disbelief: "No, you are joking. It's not true."

And he said in that emphatic slow voice he had used about his disease and the drug: "Oh, yes. I did seduce my sisters. Both of them."

Chapter

Eleven

When I got back to Linden Gardens and entered the house, I met Mr. Sewell in the hall.

"You don't even come home with the cows any more," he remarked. "The milkman's come and gone. Is this a time to get home?"

"As you see," I said.

"Lord, you people, the lives you lead," he said. "I'll reduce your rent by half because you don't wear out the sheets. What's he got that I haven't got? Gives you black crêpe-de-Chine sheets, or what, does he?"

"Yes," I said.

"Had a good night, had you? Never slept a wink?" he asked.

"Yes," I said.

"Lord," he remarked, and began to sing: *"The blushing bride she looks divine, the bridegroom he is doing fine, I'd rather have his job than mine, when I'm cleaning windows,"* and he added, "And this reminds me. There's a window broken downstairs. The wife told me to see about it. And now I've got to feed the blasted cat. Come down with me and I'll give you a cup of coffee. As a reward. Because you make me remember things. That's all I can do nowadays. Just remember."

I laughed and followed him down the stairs to the basement and into the kitchen, where we found Miss Smythe, the lecturer in philosophy, who was a privileged boarder. She was not only allowed to use the kitchen on Sundays, as we others were, but on weekdays, too. I was not jealous of her preferment, though; with her regular, heavy-jowled face and her downwards-sloping eyelids, she reminded me of a bloodhound, and because of this resemblance I was convinced that she was an utterly loyal, faithful, self-sacrificing person, deserving any such privilege.

She was cleaning sprouts and dropping them one by one into a pan with water. Clearly, her philosophy did not reach far enough to tell her that cleaning the lot at one go, and then dropping them in, would have saved her many unnecessary movements.

A half-eaten orange lay beside the peelings on the table. I said, "The orange was created by God, in ready-made slices, to be eaten by people with large families. How's that for teleology?"

She said, "Teleology is very much in fashion again, whether you like it or not."

"I don't," I said.

"Stop nattering, you two," said Mr. Sewell, getting the tin with the coffee from the shelf.

"Why don't you do some work?" Miss Smythe asked me. "I could get you something in research, easily."

"About the philosophic orange?" I asked.

"Yes," she said; "why don't you?"

"I don't feel like it," I said.

"You two get me all mixed up with my measuring and counting out the spoons," said Mr. Sewell. "This girl here is enough to turn anybody's head, on her own. And now the two of you. But I understand her. It's the same with me. I work and I drink. And when work interferes with my drink, I stop work. Only with her, it's not drink."

Miss Smythe sighed and went on cleaning the sprouts.

"Goody, goody," said Mr. Sewell, "now it's on the boil. Now

we'll get the cat's dinner ready. That's what I came down here for."

After rubbing his hands in a show of delighted anticipation, he opened a tin of sardines and laid them out on a plate, arranging them in a most meticulous fashion, with their tails in the centre, so as to form a star.

"And now for it," he said, once more rubbing his hands. He fetched from the shelf a bottle with Worcestershire sauce and dripped the inky liquid over the fish with loving care, streaking it in a criss-cross pattern.

"Oh, no," I cried.

"Oh, yes," he said; "my wife tells me to feed the cat. So I feed the cat."

Miss Smythe was still shaking her head when the black cat appeared on the outside ledge, put her head through the jagged hole in the pane and slid on to the kitchen sill.

"My heart stood still," I said. "I didn't think it could be done. I thought she'd be cut and bleed to death."

"You don't know cats," said Mr. Sewell. "Takes more than a broken window to get them down."

We all watched the cat as she jumped on to the table, lowered her head, paused with the finicky, suspicious hesitation peculiar to her kind, and then started to feed.

"Unbelievable," I said.

"Never mind," said Mr. Sewell. "I'll try cayenne pepper on her next time."

And while he went into the scullery to fetch cups and saucers, I said to Miss Smythe, "I hope that cat lives for ever. Better the cat than— Marriage is a ghastly business."

"I wouldn't know," she said; "but I suppose he should clear out."

"He'd only find himself another cat to feed," I said.

Mr. Sewell returned.

"You are a defeatist, aren't you?" she remarked.

"Mm," I said.

I went to see Gordon that evening, and he told me he had nearly taken a two-room flat in Welbeck Street. "When I told her I must have a couch in one room, she said she'd put the divan from the bedroom there. And when I asked her, does it strike you as so extraordinary that I want a bed in the bedroom? she couldn't see it. You see how it is, my poor child. I must get a proper place with a waiting room, porter, the lot. Crombie again sent me two more patients today. I can't carry on as I am now."

"That's very nice," I said. "Crombie sounds awfully decent."

"And when I get established," Gordon said. "I'll buy you that dress you wanted the other day."

"I didn't say I wanted it," I said.

"But you looked at it," he said, "though you never look at hats."

"No, naturally," I said, "I can't really wear a hat with my high plaits."

"But if you would wear a hat," he said, "what sort of a hat would you like?"

"A small hat with a short veil," I said; "just a veil to cover the eyes. I think that's frightfully becoming."

"That's what I wanted to hear," he said, "a hat like the woman wore in your dream, didn't she?" and he looked at me with delight.

"Yes," I said, "she did have on exactly that sort of hat. But it didn't suit her. She was terribly dowdy. I told you."

"I knew straightaway there was something in that hat with the veil," he said. "Now, why do you want a hat with a veil?"

"I just told you," I said. "You are frightfully dense. Because it's so becoming."

"What does a hat with a veil make you think of?" he asked.

"Nothing special," I said.

"Don't say 'special,' say 'especial,' " he said.

"Yes," I said.

"Well?" he asked.

"A veil of tears," I said; "when you weep, your eyes get shrouded with a veil of tears."

"Don't start making things up," he said.

"I'm not making it up," I said; "you asked me what it reminded me of and I told you."

"Stop running away from me," he said, and, leaning forwards, he put his hand round my elbow, with the thumb pressing into the tender inside of the bend. "I'll help you to your veil of tears," he remarked; "I'll give you something to weep about. Come on, now."

I never knew how he sorted out my replies. Why one utterance was "now we are getting somewhere," and why another was "stop making it up." I did not lie to him; I had only once lied to him deliberately, when he had struck me in the face. As far as I knew, all my replies were truthful; they seemed truthful to me in the same way as salt and sugar look the same, and yet he somehow not only saw what I said but tasted it as well, and found it salty or sweet.

"All right," I said sullenly, "but it's silly. My mother always had these hats with short veils. She looked enchanting in them, really seductive, with the eyes behind that black trellis. And I always wanted to have one like that, too. Which was ridiculous of me, I know."

"That's better," he said.

"I'm so glad," I said arrogantly.

"You wanted to be like your mother," he said. "As enchanting."

"Yes, naturally," I said. "I wanted to be as good as she was. I don't mean good in virtue. I mean, as grown-up and as seductive and as attractive to men. Which I couldn't be, of course. It was childish."

"Let's take it literally," he said. "You call it childish. Already as a child you wanted to be as attractive as your mother."

"Yes," I said.

He released my arm and leaned back in his chair. He looked pleased.

"Do you know who that woman was, in your dream?" he asked. "It was you."

"No," I cried, jumping up from the settee, "it couldn't be. I'm five feet. And she was frightfully tall, like a guardsman. And bony. And ugly."

"And she looked like O'Teague and had on a hat with a veil," he said. "The veil to you means you want to be as good as someone you admire. You want to be like O'Teague, as smart and as sophisticated, and to mix with his crowd of film actors and producers, as an equal. But you can't. Compared to him, you are provincial and frumpy and dowdy. They never talk to you when you sit with them, do they? They just tolerate you. And he doesn't talk to you, either, while they're there. He gossips films with them. And you are left out. You said, in your dream, the woman was trying so hard it was pathetic. You are trying so hard it's pathetic. That's what your dream showed you."

He was silent for a while. He was watching me.

"Yes," I said, putting a hand over my eyes.

"But that's only the beginning," he said; "we'll go a bit deeper than that."

"I don't want to," I said. "It's—it's unpleasant."

"That's the beauty of it," he remarked; "that's why it gives me such tremendous pleasure."

He got up and went to the cupboard and then joined me on the settee, placing a tin box next to him.

"Come," he said; "here is something to cheer you up," and he held a biscuit out to me.

As I wanted to take it, he raised it out of my reach. I made a lunge at it; he put his arm behind him and evaded me again. I flung myself at him and he seized me and took possession of me.

We left his place at eight o'clock and walked down Wigmore Street. I did not ask him where we were going. He liked a change of pubs and often took me to new places. Ground down by his love-making as I was, I was not in a curious frame of mind.

"You are very silent," he remarked.

"Yes," I said.

"Would you rather have had the biscuit?" he asked.

"No," I said.

"Have you seen O'Teague today?" he asked.

"Yes," I said.

"Say anything?" he asked.

"They were talking about the Heath trial and killings and murders," I said, "and when the others left to get back to their studios and back to cutting and editing and looking at the rushes, I was alone with him, and he said what a fool Heath was. And other killers like him. That if he wanted to kill someone, he'd do it without getting up from his chair. Just by wishing it."

"Ah, yes," said Gordon; "and then cast a spell on Scotland Yard so that they wouldn't arrest him."

I laughed.

"Anything else?" asked Gordon.

"He said he's not as ignorant of himself as other people. He can feel his hair grow and his nails grow, and sometimes his arms and legs are away from him, they feel separate, and he has to get them together when he wants to get up," I said.

"Very familiar," remarked Gordon. "He's pre-psychotic."

"What's that?" I asked.

"You needn't know," said Gordon. "Let's go up here and try this one," and, turning into Marylebone Lane, he entered a pub.

"Nice, old-fashioned, God-fearing, the way you like it," he remarked. "Sit down and I'll go up to the tabernacle and get some spiritual refreshment."

When he returned with the drinks, he said, "I went to the Belgrave Park Hotel the other night."

"Did you really," I exclaimed.

"Yes," he said. "I wanted to see it for myself. It's not at all as you described it."

"Isn't it?" I asked.

"No," he said; "it's just a dusty, antiquated, badly run old joint which was never grand and never smart, not even in the glorious old days. The aged grandeur, the old-fashioned elegance, that's how you said it was. That's how you see it. Your dream is full of deceit, of double-crossing, of doubts, of fear of finding out what you don't want to know. And yet you've known it for a long time. You knew quite well that O'Teague is a fake. That he's never done anything worthwhile. Where are the films he's done? Who's ever heard of him? He's not Irish, either; he's an Australian, I found that out, but that's neither here nor there. You knew his line of patter was rubbish, didn't you? You knew and you didn't want to know. You wanted to cling on."

"He's so beautiful," I said.

"That's not the reason for it," said Gordon; "and you didn't only know that he's a fake with his magic. You even knew that he's quite a stereotyped fake. Not a grain of anything original there."

"You said that," I remarked. "You. Not me. You said you knew it all by heart."

"But you knew it all by heart, too, my poor child," he said.

"What did you talk about first thing I met you? In front of the antique shop? What came to your mind?"

"The fairy-tales about the mirrors," I said, "and the man who didn't cast a shadow."

"And why were they so familiar to you?" asked Gordon. "Why were they foremost in your mind?"

I said, "Because, if you must know, I'd been reading them up, on purpose."

"And why had you been reading them up?" he asked. "Because you wanted to see where he got it from. Because that was his line of blarney. By the way, did he tell you, too, that he doesn't cast a shadow if he doesn't want to?"

"Yes," I said, "and it's out of Chamisso—of the German Romantic movement. The book is called *Peter Schlemihl*. And most of the mirror stuff is E. T. A. Hoffmann—that's about the same period, too."

Gordon said, "A humdrum psycopath with a pretty taste in literature. So you've known it all along."

"All right. I've known it all along," I said listlessly.

"And yet," said Gordon, "you come and say he's the great love of your life. And you had to work so hard at it, my poor child. But it's almost over now. You've almost come to the end. Do you want to have another drink? It might do you good. There's not much fight in you today, is there?"

"I don't want any more to drink," I said.

He said, "I'll get myself another whisky, a double, and I might not see my own shadow, either. Who knows? I'll try it," and he rose.

"I hope it chokes you," I said.

"Truth does rather choke, doesn't it?" he remarked.

When he returned, he took a gulp, smacked his lips with exaggerated cheerfulness and said, "Ah, that's fine. I feel so good and you are so languid, my sweet child." And leaning back luxuriously on the wooden settee as though it were one of the well-stuffed chairs at Shepherds, he asked casually, without glancing at me, "Tell me. Why don't you ever talk about your father?"

I struggled for breath. I was labouring under the purely bodily sensation of having my lungs congested, a sensation I had often experienced when plunging into the icy waters of the lakes in the Salzkammergut.

"Because there's nothing to talk about," I said breathlessly, and I rose from my seat, just as I would have risen out of the chill water. In my haste to get away I knocked into the table.

"Sit down," he said; "you're upsetting my drink. Don't annoy me."

I sat down.

"But there's nothing to talk about," I repeated; "I never knew him. I only met him once, when I was nineteen."

"Rubbish," he said. "You did know him! How old were you when he left you?"

"Four years," I said; "but he didn't really leave us. My mother left him, because she couldn't stick him. She took me and we went to live at my grandmother's."

"But up till then he lived with you and your mother?" he asked.

"Yes," I said.

"And you can't remember him?" he asked.

"No, of course not," I said. "I was too small."

"Fiddlesticks," said Gordon. "Of course you can remember him."

"No, I can't, I tell you!" I cried.

"Don't shout," he said. "Take a deep breath and steady yourself. Why are you so upset?"

I did not speak.

"You'd be amazed," he remarked, "what I could make you remember."

I did not reply.

"Well?" he asked.

"Nobody ever talked about him," I said. "I only know bits from my cousin Sylvia. Her father and mine were brothers. Their mother was killed by lightning. She was inside the house, mind you, opening a door. She was struck through the metal door-knob."

"You feel a bit shattered, don't you?" he asked.

"Yes," I said.

"As though you'd been struck by lightning?" he said.

"Yes."

"And all because I asked you such a simple friendly question. A father is such a friendly person, after all. Or isn't he?"

"I've no idea," I said.

"Didn't you ever enquire after him?" asked Gordon.

"Never."

"Why? Weren't you curious?"

"I wasn't."

"Do you think that's quite normal?"

"Why not?" I asked.

"Are you going to tell me," he said, "that you, a child of more than average intelligence, never wanted to find out about your own father?"

"I never wanted to," I said.

"And you've gone through life for twenty-eight years and you've never been interested in him?" he asked. "Does that strike you as natural?"

"I never gave it a thought."

"How old was your father when you were born?" he asked.

"Forty-one."

"So he is nearly seventy now, is he?"

"Yes," I said.

"Where does he live?"

"In Vienna," I said; "and I hope the weather keeps fine for him."

He said, "But when you told me about your great-grandmother and her disgusting yellow wrinked hand, you had a very good memory, I must say. And that happened when you were four. And yet you say you can't remember your father. Nothing at all?"

"No," I said. "I can't even remember what he looked like."

"And didn't you ever try to imagine what he looked like?" he asked.

"No."

"You did imagine him," said Gordon; "you knew he was old and you liked to think he was beautiful. Old and beautiful. We are back where we started. Old and beautiful."

"If you say it once more, I'm going to scream," I said.

"We'll go and eat now," he said, "and then I'll put you to bed. No sex and no cruelty, of course."

Chapter

Twelve

"What have you got against your father?" asked Gordon when I saw him on the following evening.

"He never wanted me," I said. "When my mother left and we went to live with my grandmother, he never even enquired after me. The first year he sent me a book for my birthday. And then nothing any more."

"What is he?" asked Gordon.

"He is a doctor of physics," I said. "He's got some very rare degrees. But he's never done anything with it. He's queer. Eccentric. He doesn't care about making money or going to parties, or entertaining. He's always been frigid and arrogant and difficult, my cousin Sylvia told me. And she also told me that he got a prize from the Emperor Franz-Josef for being the most brilliant pupil of the year in the Austrian Empire, or something."

"So he is distinguished, is he?" Gordon remarked. "And still you are not interested."

"No," I said; " 'If he be not fair to me, what care I how fair he be.' It's like that."

"Then you do mind about him," remarked Gordon; "you mind very much that he never wanted to see you."

"I never think about it. And anyway, before, I sometimes thought my mother did it on purpose, that she kept me away from him, because she was spiteful. But my mother was not to blame, after all, because he really couldn't have cared less for me.

When I was nineteen, I stayed in Vienna with friends of our family and they said I should meet him. That it was the right thing to do. They got in touch with him and he refused to see me, and they pestered him for quite some time—they only told me this afterwards—till he agreed. So there."

"And what was it like when you met him?" he asked.

"Nothing much," I said; "a complete stranger. Good manners, correct bearing, silent and frosty. He took me to see a skating performance—that was on ice, too. And he took me so that he wouldn't have to talk to me."

"And you would have liked him to be kind, wouldn't you?" said Gordon.

"Don't be idiotic," I said. "He was a strange gent with cold fishy eyes. Blue eyes like a carp. And I didn't want anything from him. I didn't care."

"That's what you want to believe," said Gordon; "that's what you have been telling yourself all these years, that you didn't want him and you didn't care. It was sour grapes, wasn't it?"

"I don't know," I said.

"You did know," said Gordon; "and that's why you never let yourself think about him. The thought would have been unbearable. From the very beginning, when I met you, every time I mentioned the word 'father,' you were up in arms."

"Was I?"

"You certainly were, my poor child. The first night you were here, in this room, and I mentioned the word 'father,' you wanted to do me an injury. And the other evening in the pub, when I first asked you point-blank about him, it was touch-and-go and you were running away, weren't you? It was just lucky you were still so weak from the hour before, when you didn't get the biscuit."

I did not reply.

"We'll go back to O'Teague now," he said, smiling.

"Thank God for it," I remarked; "anything to get away from this father business."

Gordon said, "O'Teague comes along, for two days, and then drifts off. Then nothing for three years. So, on one hand, there's your father—old, eccentric, peculiar, distinguished and unknown. You wanted him and couldn't get him. He's somewhere, but he is not to be got at."

"That's true," I said, "I don't even know his address."

Gordon continued, "On the other hand, there's O'Teague. Old, perhaps distinguished, peculiar, eccentric, unknown. You want him and you can't get him. You don't know anything about him. He's somehwere but he can't be got at."

He leaned forwards from his chair and took hold of both my wrists.

"Why didn't you want to sleep with O'Teague when you first met him?"

"I told you, I don't know," I said.

"And three years later you were all aflame and burning for him," he said, and, still holding my wrists, he placed my hands on his knees and held them there. "O'Teague wouldn't have worked for you if you hadn't had to fret for him and search for him and been in uncertainty over him, for three years. It's that three years' absence, the seeking for the great, distinguished, eccentric old man, that turned him into the love of your life. But of course all he was was a flimsy, shabby, third-rate copy of your father."

"You've been inventing it, it's not true!" I cried.

He took my legs between his knees and held them tightly clamped.

He said, "And when you got hold of O'Teague, you wouldn't let go. You knew by then that he was claptrap and a fake, but he fitted the bill so well, didn't he? The great unknown, found at last. Why were you hiding him from me? Why were you so afraid I'd find out? 'A man I happen to know.' Just like this. What did you have to hide? You don't even sleep with him. But so sham he couldn't stand up to be looked at in the light of day."

I had been trying to hide my face from his glance, and as I could not get away from his clasp, I put my head on his knees.

"You can go to Delmain's tomorrow," he said, "and the day after."

I shook my head and said, with my voice muffled against his trouser-legs: "No, I can't. I couldn't stand it."

"My sweet child. You don't know the pleasure you are giving me. I'll let you get up now. We'll go out. But go and make loo-loo first."

It was in the beginning of October when I decided to order a coat and skirt at a tailor's off Bond Street, one of those of whom it is said, "If you ask how much he charges, it means you can't afford him." I could not afford him, and yet I did it. I was feeling prodigal out of the marvellous relief that Gordon had dealt with Derek O'Teague, and without being disgusted with me during the procedure.

It must have been at this time, when I had been Gordon's mistress for about four months, that he took a new interest in my "making loo-loo."

From the first night I spent with him in Portman Square, he had continued to remind me about it, telling me it was time I went to the bathroom.

But now, on such occasions, he would engage me in talk, and as I went to the bathroom he would follow me, stopping at the open door, and continue talking while watching me, as though unwilling to have the conversation interrupted.

Then when he did not halt at the door but was on the point of following me right into the bathroom, I stopped him, saying, "You are not to come with me."

He leaned his head against the door-post, beat the wall with his fists and groaned, "You want to punish me again. You always want to punish me."

I was delighted, as I always was at his play-acting, and laughed.

But the next time he came inside with me and planted himself in front of me as I was sitting down.

After this I made a few more attempts to make him refrain from this new habit, but I could not shift him. I got used to having him stand there, observing me closely. His interest grew more advanced. It did not stop at watching me; he started to make remarks about it. At first he did this only while we were in the bathroom; later on it became a topic to which he kept returning, while, for instance, we were walking in the street on our way to a pub.

He made remarks like: "Why do you have to do it like a horse, in one big stream? It's so crude. I think I should fit you with a button and then you'd do it more daintily, in four runlets," or "Why are you always in such a hurry over it? You want to get it over and done with. Why don't you do it more gently, more gracefully, and with the refinement of leisure?"

This did not make me feel offended. I was sure that I was performing this function in no way different from other women. But I did consider Gordon's preoccupation with unease. He was clearly spellbound and enchanted by the way I did it. On the other hand, he tried to hide his enchantment by offering his remarks in a detached, humorous manner, as though fully aware of how ridiculous they were, as though bringing out these bizarre conceits in order to make me shocked and indignant.

I refused to be shocked; I pretended to be amused. I also pretended to be amused when, one evening in Frith Street, I stumbled and nearly fell over and caught his arm to steady myself, and he remarked, "You want to break your leg just to embarrass me."

At that time Gordon developed a preference for Soho, which I shared; I liked to show him the pubs which I knew so well from my days with Reggie Starr, such as the Wheat Sheaf, the Bricklayers, the Fitzroy, the French House, the Swiss House, and the Dog and Duck.

It was in Frith Street, too, that one night, after having left the Dog and Duck in Bateman Street, round the corner, Gordon returned to his favourite subject and said, "I am sure you'd like to make loo-loo now. Why don't you?"

"How can I?" I said. "Anyway, it'll keep till we get back."

"No, it won't," he said; "you must do it now. There's nobody about," and he gave me a look as though delighted at his own whimsy.

It was getting on towards eleven, it was a dark night, but in Soho the streets are never deserted.

"I wouldn't dream of it," I said, still laughing. But I was uneasy.

He turned serious. He said, "Do as I tell you."

"I'm hanged if I will," I said. "I could even get myself arrested for it."

He said, "Don't annoy me. You know it doesn't pay," and as I looked at him, speechless, he added in a low voice bleached with rage, "Go on. Here in this doorway. I'll stand in front of you."

The tone of his voice made me submit. I entered the doorway of an old house from which a passage opened on to a courtyard, squatted down close to the ground and did what he wanted me to do.

He was in front of me, blotting out my sight, with his back turned towards me.

Suddenly, I heard him say in a pleasant, jovial tone of voice, "Oh, good evening, Constable."

I caught my breath with fright.

He said without turning round, "Go on. It was only a joke."

A few days after this, again in Frith Street, again after closing time at the pubs, he merely said, "Come along, my poor child," and took me by the wrist. This time, though, he did not stop by the doorway but led me straight into the courtyard.

It was a most unsavoury place, as far as one could see by the spare light which penetrated from the lamps on the street beyond; two or three windows in the upper floors showed their oblongs of dull gold, secretive and self-contained behind curtains.

The aged, obscene body of the building was bursting open with sores and splitting with wounds. Dustbins welling over with the pus of garbage, heaps of rubble and planks like smashed bones and broken teeth, crates oozing tumbled junk were ranged against the walls where the plaster, patchy and peeling like eczematous skin, revealed the crumbling brickwork. The ground was slippery and slimy, as though it had been excreting its own filth.

"Go on," he said, "here, against this wall. That's a very cosy place," and he walked with me towards a corner.

I crouched down and he stood in front of me, watching me, wordless.

When I had finished and was about to straighten up and tidy my underwear, he moved close to me, pushed me into the corner, twisted my free arm behind me, and pressed me violently against the wall. I was gripping my handbag, which I did not dare to drop on the disgustingly soiled ground. When I decided to let go of my bag and got the arm free, for fending him off, he seized my hand and held it against my breast, bending my arm; he kept it pinned there with the weight of his body.

I struggled in silence, not daring to make a sound for fear of attracting someone's attention, and during my struggle he forced and pushed me lower down so that I was half crouching again. My knees fell apart and he raped me, with my head and shoulders grating against the rough wall.

He achieved his satisfaction in perhaps two minutes, in a time-span even shorter than when he had taken me on the garden bench.

When he let go of me, he straightened up, turned his back on me and began to pace round the yard.

I picked up my handbag and arranged my clothes, while he moved about at random, raising his eyes to the jagged roof-and-chimney line, like a tourist keenly absorbed in sightseeing.

I remained standing in my corner till he happened to pass nearby.

"Shall we go?" he asked, coming to a halt.

"Yes," I said.

"Whatever you say, my sweet child."

We walked slowly under the archway, into the passage and out on to the pavement.

We waited in silence for some ten minutes at a bus stop in Regent's Street till, getting impatient, he hailed a cab. When we got to his place, I followed him into the room with my coat on, undecided about what to do.

"Get undressed and lie down," he said.

To my surprise, my clothes were not as soiled as I had expected them to be. Only the edge of my coat was begrimed in one place, and my stockings were laddered. One leg of my panties had a torn elastic and I had lost the metal loop of a suspender. I did have my pair of black kid gloves, though. I found them neatly folded in the pocket of my coat. I must have placed them there before crouching down. I was empty of all emotion.

All I could think of was to congratulate myself on the possession of my gloves and to be glad that I had not been wearing the curly, white lambskin coat I was so fond of.

"Can I have a bath?" I asked, sitting down on the settee.

I had never yet taken a bath in Gordon's place because he never allowed me to wash between my thighs.

"No," he said; "you want to deprive me of what belongs to me. You can wash your hands, but you're not to wash anywhere else. Leave the bathroom door open so that I can see you."

When I returned, he told me to go to bed.

I lay down submissively, and when he took me, he made me cry out with bliss, as he went on in his slow, steady, relentless way, and I received him with sighs and trembling.

Afterwards I remained spread out on my back and with my eyes closed, and he drew the pins out of my hair and laid them on the bedside table and unfurled my plaits.

"You must have lost some of your knives and daggers, my poor child," he remarked; "they're not such a handful as usual."

I did not reply.

He said, "We'd better go back there, tomorrow, and look for them. What do you say?"

I cried, "No, I won't go to the cemetery again!"

"Why was it like a cemetery?" he asked. "No, don't turn your head away. I want to undo your hair."

"God knows," I remarked; "I just said it like that, without thinking."

"Then say more without thinking," he said. "Keep your head still, my poor child. Why was it like the cemetery?"

"I've no idea," I said. "I suppose all the rubbish and rubble. Like a graveyard full of broken bones."

He said, "Have you ever seen a graveyard with broken bones lying about?"

"No, they are always beautifully tidy and well kept."

"Then why do you serve me up with this nonsense?" he asked. "Stop running away from me. Why was it like a cemetery?"

"Because it was so slithery and squashy," I said. "If you were to tread on slugs, it would feel beastly, just like it."

"So it would," he said; "go on."

I said, "It's only that Miss Smythe the other day—but that's got nothing to do with it."

"That's better," he said. "I always like it when it's got nothing to do with it. Go on."

"She told me a funny story," I said, "about when she was staying somewhere in Burgundy, before the war. At that inn they gave her a dish of snails and she didn't like them; they were frightfully garlicky, and she only had a few, and then the waitress came and said to her, 'But you must eat them, they're specially good, I picked them specially this morning from my mother's grave.' "

"Don't say 'specially,' say 'especially,' " he said.

"Yes," I said, "and that's all. And it isn't funny, of course. It's really shocking."

He said, "So you feel I took you to the cemetery and violated you on your mother's grave. That's what you wanted, isn't it?"

I opened my eyes.

He was observing me.

"It's not true," I said. "What's my mother got to do with it? Why do you always have to say these beastly things?"

"I am a brute, am I?" he asked.

"Yes, you are," I said, "and I'd have to be mad to want anything like it."

"But you do want it, and you are not mad," he said, smiling; "it's only one of your phantasies. But what would you say if a girl really did that sort of thing? Why would you say she was doing it?"

"How do I know?" I said. "And why should I tell you? You tell me. You are always so clever."

"Don't hide your face," he said, "I want you to say it yourself. Come on," and he slapped my arm.

"Out of revenge, of course," I said, "and out of spite. Though it would be idiotic, really. Because the mother is dead— naturally—or there wouldn't be her grave to perform on—so how can you revenge yourself on someone who's dead? Anyway, it's got nothing to do with me."

"But your mother is dead, too," he remarked.

"So she is," I said; "so what?"

"You may well say, so what," he said. "Your mother is dead, but you still behave as though she were alive. Sometimes you want to placate her, and do things which would please her, and sometimes you want to get back at her and spite her. You are like a child that whistles in the dark. As though the dark cared, my poor child, as though the dark cared."

"This is absurd," I said.

"No, it isn't," he remarked, "because I know why you want to revenge yourself on your mother."

"But she's never done anything bad to me," I said.

"Oh, yes, she has."

"That's not true," I said; "she was always frightfully decent to me, and when I wanted to borrow her sables for the opera, she always let me have them. You know nothing about her. I should know better than you do."

"You do know better," he said; "that is, you do know it better than I do. Much better. But you won't admit it."

"I can't think what you mean."

"Because you don't want to think," he remarked.

"Leave me alone," I said.

"I'll leave you alone when you've told me," he said.

"You can't drag me along like this. I won't be dragged and forced into saying something when I'm innocent and never did it."

"The more you run away, the nearer you are getting. You just now had to tell me that you won't be dragged, and that you didn't do it. But you were dragged, against your wish, and you didn't do it, either. When you were four years old and your mother took you away from your father. Did she or didn't she?"

"Yes, she did," I said.

"And you've never forgiven her, have you?" he asked.

I rolled over and hid my face in the nest of my folded arms. He took me round the waist and round my hips and returned me to my back, as before.

I kept my eyes shut, and he laid the strands of my hair over my shoulders and spread them down my sides. I opened my eyes and saw my bare breasts rising like pale sandbanks from the dark waters of a river. He lay down, supporting himself on one elbow.

He said, "I'll hold you for ever. Because I shall always find new ways of torturing you."

I made no reply.

"You are very silent," he remarked.

"Yes," I said.

"My sweet child."

Chapter

Thirteen

A few days after this, when I arrived in Portman Square at six in the afternoon, Gordon told me he had been asked that night to a party by Leonie Beck and that she had said he could bring me along, too.

"Oh, I wish you'd phoned up and told me before," I said, "and I'd have put on something decent."

"It won't be that sort of party," he said.

Even without his reassuring remark I would have been content as it was.

I knew Leonie Beck slightly, and I was aware that there is a way of insulting people by under-dressing for their parties; and I was pleased at the thought that I was not even wearing a dress but was clad in a pale blue cotton blouse buttoned with mother-of-pearl, a tartan skirt in scarlet, yellow and pale blue, snub-toed scarlet shoes with a matching bag, and the white fur coat.

That I liked the idea of insulting Leonie Beck was unjustified, considering that she had behaved very nicely to me on the two previous occasions when I had met her.

She was a friend of Gordon's and devoted entirely to the practice of psychoanalysis. She was from Berlin, in her late thirties, and single. With her big bust and full arms, she had that kind of plumpness which carries an aura of being well fed and affluent. She had a broad, flat face with a tiny nose, and large-waved hair bleached to the colour of yellowish ivory; and her Pekinese dog

did not only show in his mask a desperate likeness to her countenance, but his coat was so exactly matched in hue to her hair that
he could have furnished his mistress with a wig. Her dresses
were richly pleated and gathered to disguise the heaviness of her
bosom and her hips, and she loved those jewellers' gadgets
which I detested, such as gilt pegs worn over a cardigan to prevent it slipping off her shoulders, or a gold contraption shaped
like a giant paper-clip with which she attached her gloves to her
handbag.

I admired her on principle, as a succesful career-woman, just
as I admired the loyal Miss Smythe. Gordon said that she was
"not too bad" in her profession and that she "got through by being motherly." He sometimes went to concerts with her; they
both liked the modern serious music for which I had no love and
no understanding.

He had simply introduced me as "Louisa" without giving any
explanations. He would, I imagined, have cut off her enquiries
about me in the same way as he had done that evening off the
Cromwell Road, by telling the truth and making it sound like a
joke—that he had first got to know me on a garden bench.

Leonie Beck's behaviour towards me was pleasant and un-
forced, with that touch of solicitous and caring motherliness
which was her business asset. Every time I made an utterance—
and I made only a few obvious ones—she cooed her approval
and understanding, glazed with a sugar-icing of wisdom.

For instance, she mentioned that she had cured herself of mi-
graines by cutting chocolate out of her diet, and I, trying to be
pleasant, hastened to say that I knew how prostrating attacks of
this ailment could be, as my mother had suffered from them, too.

She said, "How nice of you to be so sympathetic. Migraine is
one of those ills where the body has to bear patiently what the
soul cannot carry."

I refrained from asking her why in her case it had been the chocolate, and in my mother's case, the burdened soul.

Or she would admire spontaneously my red shoes: "Such a cheerful colour, so refreshing in all the drabness around one," after which she drew me into the women's league against men: "But of course, Richard doesn't appreciate it. Or does he, I wonder?"

Yes, she called him Richard. The audacity took my breath away the first time I heard it, and I had to go through what my cinematic friends at Delmain's called a "double-take" before my amazement vanished.

Thus, after my first shock of "how dare she," I recalled myself to order and had to admit that to refer to him as Richard was the most natural mode of address. What else should she have called him? And yet, despite this reasoning with myself, I could not understand how she could be so insensitive to what Gordon was. But what was he?

To me he was the frightening, sinister, implacable, and exacting taskmaster; his looks and his cast of mind were sardonic, like those of Mephisto, whose amusement is based on destroying comforting beliefs and inflicting pain—in the true sense of the word "sardonic," which derives from the name of a poisonous herb that, when taken, produces spasms of the face which counterfeit the look of smiling cheerfulness.

Moreover, to my mind, Gordon's power was so strong that I could not believe in his case that, as people say, "it takes two to play the game," by which I meant that I was sure he could have enslaved any woman he chose. And it was because of this conviction that I was astonished that Leonie Beck failed to grasp at least the potential menace of his spell.

Apart from such considerations, I did not pay much attention to Gordon's talk with her. It touched on topics that did not interest me: meetings of committees and meetings of a society, names of consultants, new appointments, the book Dr. Crombie was about to publish in a new and enlarged edition, and Gordon's work at what he liked to call "the Nervous Hospital for West End Diseases."

Only once did the Pekinese create a diversion, during a walk in the park, by refusing to move away from a tree, and Leonie Beck said with a sigh and a smile, "Unfortunately, he's got a mother-fixation on me. He refuses the company of other dogs."

"You mean, of other bitches," remarked Gordon.

I burst out laughing, while she, smiling indulgently at my merriment, said, turning to Gordon, "Just now I'm treating a very sad case of it. Fifty years old, homosexual, of course, and sleeps every night in the double-bed with his eighty-year-old mother."

Later, when we were alone, I asked Gordon, "Why 'homosexual, of course'? Why couldn't he do it properly and sleep with someone, a woman, who's at least a bit *like* his mother?" And Gordon said, "That's right. At least a bit like her. You are a sheer joy, my sweet child."

The night of the party, Gordon was in an easy, relaxed frame of mind. He said we would be going out soon, have drinks and dinner, and then go on to Leonie Beck's flat.

He was pacing about the room, as he often did when he was not questioning me, and telling me about a new patient: "He's a young man, a very gay spark. Given the choice between treatment or prison, because his people are rich. As you know, justice is equal for the rich and the poor. He's been masquerading as a wing commander, complete with medals for distinguished service, and running up bills at the Berkeley and the Ritz. Great sense of humour. He was born ten months after his brother, and his mother didn't want him."

He paused, looked out of the window, turned round, and

added, "No child likes to feel unwanted. People do queer things in grown-up life to make up for it."

I kept silent.

He continued, "I think I'll shove him on to Bruce. I'm getting fed up with him. I saw Bruce the other day. He's disgusted with the outcome of the Heath trials. All the expert evidence good for nothing; it's wasted on the jury of twelve English grocers good and true, and on the judge, too. They say, if he didn't know what he was doing, then he's insane. And if he knew what he was do-ing, then he's sane. What they can't understand is that he knew exactly what he was doing and at the same time couldn't stop himself doing it. If people only realised—oh, what's the use of talking! We do because we must. And just now, we must go and eat. Get your things on, my poor child. But go and make loo-loo first."

He took me to Soho, to an Italian restaurant in Greek Street where we had not been for many weeks.

He ordered *bolito misto*, which we both liked, with beef, chicken, tongue, sausage, carrots and potatoes, all bland and boiled, enlivened with thick green sauce full of spicy chopped herbs. To follow we had Bel Paese; it was tired and elderly, and when Gordon had eaten his cheese, I put my unfinished slice on his plate.

He ate it, saying, "You are very much at home with me now, aren't you? Everything you don't want you shove on my plate."

"Yes," I said.

"And what's more, I take it," he added; "so that you are quite comfortable with me, aren't you, despite everything?"

"Yes," I said.

"It's not often that you are right, but this time you are wrong," he remarked. "It's not despite everything. It's because of everything."

And when I looked at him in silence, he continued, "Oh, yes. It's as bad as that. Finish your wine."

After the waiter had taken the plate with the bill and the money, Gordon said, "I must go back into analysis again."

"Why," I asked, "you? You are a doctor. You are not a patient."

"Don't talk rubbish," he said, "like that time when you thought doctors were immune from V.D."

"Yes, but—"

"But what?"

"You must be very sane and well-balanced yourself," I said, "or you couldn't treat your crackpots."

"That's like saying that Praxiteles himself must have been as beautiful as a Greek god or he couldn't have made the statue of Hermes."

"But what do you want with it?" I asked. "You've had it all. Do you want still more training?"

"No," he said, "but I must go back. I must know what is happening."

I did not understand and I did not dare to ask any further, just as I had not dared to ask him on what points we would be quarrelling if we got married. The holiday mood of easy confidences was over. It had been over already in his room, with his "We do because we must."

He remained silent till the waiter returned with the change.

I followed him to the cloakroom, where the woman attendant performed the small miracle of recall which every good restuarant provides for the gratification of its customers.

"I never understand how it's done," I exclaimed as we turned to the stairs. "How does she remember which coat is whose? And never a mistake."

"She'd be a vigorous poke, I should say," remarked Gordon,

"but coarse. Every woman is coarse as compared to you, my sweet child."

"I like your new topcoat very much," I said, flooded by the happiness his exceedingly rare compliment gave me. "Is it by the same man from Hanover Square?" I knew he had recently been to his tailors, but had only mentioned a suit he had ordered.

"From the same," he said.

We got out on the street.

"And it's given me a melancholy thought, my poor child," he added; "my last coat was good for six years. Now I've got this one. And after this—maybe there'll be one more. Maybe."

It was one of those remarks which I did understand—it was not hard to understand—but of which I could not feel the truth. It was like all the Elizabethan poetry I knew, with its whispering, murmuring, declaiming, and shrieking at the thought of approaching death, and which never touched me despite its marvellous splendour. I was too young to feel the terror of it. Besides, why should he die so soon? I asked myself. There's nothing wrong with him. And I kept silent, certain that any remark I might offer would place me among his "stupid women."

We went down Old Compton Street, which opened on to the derelict square with the bombed church in the middle.

Gordon said, "Ah, yes, the Lord our God. The only man in London who hasn't got housing trouble. I really must get myself a place to live in. Something in Harley Street, two or three rooms, with one serving as a consulting room. And then you'll come and live with me, my poor child. You'll clean the place for me and be my dogsbody."

I listened without saying yes or no. A fear gripped me, for the same reason that I had been relieved when he had told me he would not marry me.

I was afraid to live with him day by day. It was not the labour of domesticity I dreaded; I would have submitted to it, as I submitted to all his other demands. It was the fear of domesticity itself. I could not bear to be confronted by his irritation over an electric switch that had gone wrong, or a missing button on his shirt. Our whole relationship was an adventure, and like all adventures it was outside of the everyday. We were both immersed in ordinary life, where switches are out of order and buttons are missing, but only when we were not together. When I was with Gordon, I felt like the tourist in Venice who cannot and will not realise that the inhabitants of that dream city have to meet the gas bill like everybody else.

"We must have a drink first," he was saying, "to ward off the slings and arrows ahead of us. She's got no idea of decent booze. She'll give us something lady-like, probably a wine-cup with fruit in it, something harking back to the good old days in Berlin."

We entered the Swiss House.

I looked round. There was nobody there from Reggie Starr's crowd and I did not regret it. And yet, in those days when I had been with Reggie, I had always been disappointed when we had remained on our own. I had never known before the peace and contentment which Gordon gave me. Why this was so I could not understand; there was this constant stormy tension between us which flickered through our relationship like lightning in a summer sky.

"I shan't have anything," I said; "I've had a lot of wine."

Gordon ordered a double whisky.

"When do we have to be there?" I asked. "It's nearly nine o'clock now."

He croaked in the very loud voice of an irascible old general, "Do you always have to babble, woman? Do you think I'm blind? Do you think I can't read the clock, or what? I may be with one foot in the grave, but by Jove, you shan't push me in." He was greatly pleased when I blushed, and several of the guests turned from the bar counter and looked at us enquiringly and expectantly, hoping for the diversion of a shrill scene.

I started to laugh. He had not acted the deaf old general for some time, and I was glad he had abandoned his wintry thoughts.

"We'll walk up here and get a bus at the top," said Gordon as we left the Swiss House and turned into Dean Street. He took hold of my wrist.

But instead of continuing straight ahead, which would have brought us into Oxford Street and quite near to a bus stop, he took the right turn into Bateman Street, and when we found ourselves at the corner of Frith Street he turned right once more, towards Shaftesbury Avenue, instead of keeping in the direction of Oxford Street.

"No," I said. I stopped short. He twisted my arm and I gave a stifled scream. The passers-by on the other side of the pavement pursued their way, never looking round. It takes more than a low scream to draw attention in Soho.

"No, I won't," I said.

"Be quiet," said Gordon. "Men must do and women must weep." And he gave another painful twist to my arm.

We entered the archway opening into the courtyard, and this time he pressed me against a pile of planks and broken crates and held me there half sitting, half leaning.

I decided I would not fight him and get it done and over with, but I could not control myself. I was seized with a rage worse than on the previous occasion, and I struggled, if anything, more desperately than the other night. But this time more painfully, because as I tried to wrench myself from his grasp, my bones were knocked and my flesh was bruised against the jagged, angular pieces of wood on which he forced me to lean. It was as though the "cemetery" itself were assisting him in his rape, by subduing me with blows from all sides.

Again he achieved his pleasure in a minute or so, and again he moved away from me and began pacing the yard in the most unconcerned manner, contemplating the sky, the roofs, and the chimneys.

When he was at the far end of the yard, with his back turned to me, I stepped gingerly, so as to prevent my heels from clattering, to the archway, ran through the passage and out into the street, and turned towards Shaftesbury Avenue, from where I intended to get a bus.

I heard footsteps behind me; they caught up with mine. A stranger passed by and gave me a long look. I crossed to the other pavement and breathed deeply to steady the thumping of my heart. My knees were shaking so badly that they knocked together at each step.

When I reached the corner of Frith Street and Shaftesbury Avenue, the well-known grip encircled my wrist. My body ceased shaking, my fitful breathing grew even and steady, and my heart was peaceful in my breast.

"We'll pick up a cab," said Gordon; "it's getting late," and, falling into the querulous, maundering cockney voice: "Trust you to delay me. You are dreadful, you women. You're no use to any decent Christian."

He stopped a taxi, and we got in and sat in silence through the ride.

I glanced at him once, when he clicked his lighter, and I saw his profile outlined by the flame, and the sheen flickering on the gun-metal of his case. He did not offer me a cigarette.

He never offered me a cigarette; when I wanted one I had to ask him for it. And I did not carry cigarettes on me any more. He had stopped me from doing this by saying that it was unbecoming for a woman to have a packet of cigarettes in her handbag, and that he would buy me a gold case as soon as he got established in Harley Street. I did not want a gold case; I would have preferred a tortoiseshell one, mounted in gold and with a ruby clasp, to match my powder case, which my mother had given me, but I knew that when the time came he would choose what he wanted me to have.

Leonie Beck lived in Upper Harley Street, in one of those plum-coloured-brick mansions dating from the eighties of the past century.

There was an elderly porter, of the falsely cheerful kind, spry and guileful, who probably talked in the manner Gordon had assumed a few minutes ago, with his "You are dreadful, you women"; he was sitting on the well-polished bench in the hall as we entered, reading an evening paper. As we stepped into the lift, of which he was holding the scrolled-iron sliding doors open for us, he gave me a look, set his features in a rigid mask and shut his mouth tightly. It was an expression of disapproval, stifled as soon as it had arisen.

I thought that the rouge on my lips had probably got smudged over my face, and while we were riding upstairs, I hurriedly got out my little pocket mirror and glanced at myself. I was free of smudges; my mouth was faintly rouged, just as it had been when he had left the restaurant.

It was Leonie Beck herself who opened the door for us. I noticed with contemptuous satisfaction that she was dressed up for the evening. She wore black satin and was abundantly bejewelled with pearls and rhinestones. Cooing something about our being late but nevertheless most welcome, and that all the other guests were already assembled, she led us to an unsightly clothes-stand of red-lacquered wood and brass rails and a brass trough ordained to hold canes and umbrellas. It was a piece quite alien to English soil, and, curling my lips, I thought that she must have brought this treasure with her from Berlin.

"But you are in an awful state," she exclaimed, taking my coat.

I looked at Gordon, who was just slipping out of his fine dark blue topcoat with the narrow velvet collar. He was the same as I always knew him, neither different in dress nor grooming, and I was at a loss to find fault with his dark suit and tie and his habitual white shirt; I had never known him to wear any other kind of shirt. He was observing me with a smile of deep satisfaction, while Leonie Beck stood by, still holding my coat.

"But dreadful," she exclaimed in the tone of an indignant mother; "you are in a shocking state."

"Who? What?" I asked.

She put my coat on a hanger and fell to wringing her hands. "But look at yourself," she cried, still wringing her hands.

There was no mirror nearby. I raised my hand to the nape of my neck, where, I knew from experience, the rot of dishevelment always sets in. I felt a few loose strands of hair and tucked them hastily under my firmly pinned-up plaits.

"But look at yourself," she repeated urgently, impatiently, and as though horror-stricken against all belief.

I looked down my figure.

My stockings were in holes such as I had never seen before, round holes as large as desert plates, from which one of my knees protruded, indecently naked, and parts of my calves. My other knee, though covered, was streaked with dried blood. There was a tear ripped through one side of my skirt, revealing a triangle of petticoat; a piece of torn hem was flapping beneath it, and, twisting my head over my shoulder, I could perceive the hem undone as far as my eye could follow. Down in front, off centre, my petticoat was dipping below my skirt; the shoulder-strap on that side must have broken.

I bent over and rubbed some wood shavings off my knees and plucked a few splinters off my skirt. Peering over my other shoulder, I saw patches of greenish slime on the lower part of the skirt; they might have been traces of putrid vegetables.

"Where have you been? What have you been doing?" cried Leonie Beck.

I straightened up and looked at Gordon. He looked at me, his smile deepening. I tilted my head back and continued looking at him, while she repeated, "What have you been doing?"

"We've been to the cemetery," said Gordon, slowly and emphatically, without taking his eyes off me.

"To the cemetery? Is it possible? Now, at this time of night? I should have thought—" she exclaimed.

"Yes, to the cemetery," I said, lowering my eyes.

"But what am I to do with you?" she wailed tearfully.

I glanced at Gordon.

"Exactly what you asked us here for," he said. "Let's go in, shall we? Come along, my poor child."

While Leonie Beck, still flustered, went through the introductions, Gordon sat down on the low, wide window-ledge at the far end of the room, well away from the other guests, and motioned me to sit on the floor at his feet. This I did, and I remained like this for the rest of the evening.

Sitting thus close to him, separate from the others, in a position of bondage, dependence, and servitude, I was serene and appeased in my heart, just as my body had become serene and appeased as soon as Gordon had caught up with me at the corner of Frith Street and I had felt his fingers closing over my pulse.

In my delicious sense of being safe and protected, I let my

eyes roam the room at random, noting that the tables, cabinets and book-shelves were all composed of wooden red-lacquered cubes, including the flower-stands, which were built up like little flights of stairs, each small surface set with a potted cactus. It was the ugly, self-conscious *Bauhaus* tradition of the twenties which I still remembered from the flat of a cousin of my mother's who had prided himself on his avant-garde views and had been a friend of Kafka's, at a time when none of my family had ever heard of that name.

Leonie Beck came several times to our bay to see if we wanted our glasses refilled, and each time she asked me in an anxious whisper if I were feeling well. This she did, I was certain, partly out of genuine concern and partly out of spite, so as to make sure that I would continue feeling awkward, and I thought with derision how benighted she was, and that it was just because Gordon had mortified me and shown that he owned me that I was happy.

At half past eleven Gordon told me to get up.

"We must be on our way, trotting along, pushing off," he said with heavily acted joviality, giving one of his parodies of cheerfulness. "My poor child is so tired, she is quite pale," he added.

It was the first time that he had looked at me since we sat down, and I lowered my head, ashamed that he had dragged me through the filth, ashamed that he had exposed me to public view in the state of my humiliation, while in the depths of my heart there streamed the satisfaction that I was helplessly in his power.

On the following morning, after Gordon told me to get dressed and that he would see me home, I said, "But I'll have to go without stockings; it shows less that way. And I can't put on my slip underneath either, or it will dip. And I look ghastly with my hem dragging, half up and half down. But there's no help for it now."

"God looks into the heart and not at those worthless rags, my poor child," he remarked in an unctuous tone of voice quavering with emotion.

I burst into laughter. He watched me while I plaited my hair, and said: "Do you know, some time ago, I went out with Leonie Beck and got drunk. Then we went back to her place and she dragged me to bed with her. And I couldn't. I just couldn't."

"That's impossible," I cried. "You!—and couldn't?"

"No, I couldn't," he said. "I just can't stand these fat-arsed women."

"But even so, you of all people!" I said incredulously.

"She was most concerned about me," he continued; "so kind, so understanding, so sympathetic. She got on to question me, very tactfully, mind you, about my failing—oh, yes, don't laugh—and gave me to understand how sorry she was for me, and that I should be getting treatment for it."

"I'm staggered. I can't believe it," I said. "Oh, God, when I think—"

"I took it all very humbly, mind you," he said. "I hung my head and I mumbled, and I told her how miserable I was with my potency troubles. That's so. Did I ever? No, I never. Was I miserable? Proper miserable I was."

"No," I said, "I refuse to—I can't—I simply—"

I had finished building up my plaits into a crown; I turned round to look at him.

He said, gazing into space absently, and as though talking to himself, "There you are, that's life for you. To you I am a sexual monster, and to her I am impotent."

Chapter

Fourteen

It was not only my clothes but my shoes, too, which had got their share of humiliation on that night of Leonie Beck's party. The tips of my scarlet pumps were scuffed and darkened with grime, and it took me a fortnight till I found a cobbler who was willing to restore them, and another four weeks till he achieved it, by hiding the damage under rosettes of scarlet leather. It was this, he told me, the difficulty of obtaining a leather of matching colour, which had taken him so long.

It was a damp, mild, cheerless day towards the end of November when I put on my red shoes for the first time once more. Sitting on a bench in Regent's Park, I stretched my feet in front of me and said, "Look, I haven't worn them for ages. I've only got them back now, and you haven't even noticed."

"Oh yes, I have," said Gordon.

"I'm so glad I've got them again," I said; "it makes me feel like that time in Germany, when young Dent jumped on the bass-fiddle and smashed it, and when they carried it in, a week later, all repaired, and set it up on the bandstand. Dent gave a roll on the drums and we all stood up and cheered."

"Why are you so fond of your red shoes?" asked Gordon.

"Because they are so nice, so unusual," I said, still looking down at them, thinking how exactly like him that was, and how every other man by now would have remarked at my pretty feet.

"I've always been devoted to them," I added, "because they are so extravagant. But once, they nearly got me into trouble."

"What sort of trouble?" asked Gordon. "Let's get up and walk, shall we?"

"But only on the proper paths," I said, rising. "I won't have them messed up any more."

"Whatever you say, my poor child," he said, and gave me his hungry look, as though lying in wait.

I said defiantly, "I mean, I won't walk through the grass. It's so soggy."

"So it is," he said without taking his eyes off me. "Let's have it now. There is nothing more cheering than other people's troubles."

And while we started walking away from the river, and turned into a wide, straight, long-stretched avenue, I told him how I had gone with several others from our mess, among them young Captain Dent, to the Atlantic. The Atlantic was, at that time, a transit hotel for high-ranking officers, and there was dancing every night. It was a spacious, dignified hotel, designed by the same architect who had created the Ritz in London, and it bore a marked similarity to that place. Unlike the Ritz, though, and owing to its present use, it had acquired a reputation of moral laxness, and there was a story that a major-general had been woken at two o'clock one night by a knock at his door and had heard the voice of the desk-sergeant enquiring, "You got a woman in your room, sir?" and upon the shouted reply, "No, damn you!" the voice had said, "Well, here's one."

During dinner, before going out that evening, I had worn a dress, which we women were allowed to do, as long as we stayed in our own mess; then, upon deciding to go out, I had changed into my best uniform and put on pale green silk stockings, which were permitted as being a shade of khaki; and I kept on my red shoes, enchanted at the contrast they made with the green, and thinking that they would not be frowned upon in the relaxed air of the Atlantic.

I was dancing with Dent when Miss Cobb, the women's welfare officer, stepped on to the glossy floor and made straight for us. She was a short, dapper person in her fifties, with an eyeglass swinging on a black ribbon over the sagging bosom which she flattened down under the tight-fitting tunic of her excellently tailored uniform.

She brought us to a halt by seizing me by the scruff of my collar, and roared with the crudely jovial voice which she affected, "Damn you, Louisa, with your tarty shoes. And the top button of your tunic undone, too. What will you be doing next? Swishing about with your shirt open and dangling your tits like the sow in the farmyard?"

"Oh, Cobbie, be a sport," I said in my most winning way.

"Louisa hasn't got as many tits as a sow," remarked young Dent. "Think again, Cobbie, before you bark."

"You pipe down," said the welfare officer. "What do you think this is? A military mess or a brothel?"

"Heaven forbid," said young Dent with a guffaw. "You'd never make this into a paying proposition. Look around you. Nothing but climacteric women as far as the eye can see. If it were different, I'd suggest we all dance a ring-a-ring-of-roses, boys and girls, holding hands, only we wouldn't be holding hands."

"You shut your trap," said the welfare officer; "that's got nothing to do with Louisa. I've a good mind to send her home, together with her red shoes. That would learn her."

"Oh, you wouldn't," I pleaded; "you are too kind."

"Kind but firm, that's my motto," said the welfare officer,

running her hand through her short grey hair, as though undecided. "Oh, all right," she added, "but only because you've got
such pretty little feet. Get away with you now; I don't know you.
I haven't seen you," and shooting her shirt cuffs out of her
sleeves, she turned and left us.

"Very jolly, life in the army," said Gordon when I finished.

"But quite harmless, really," I hastened to say. "That was only
their *façon de parler*, you know. It's funny, though, about Dent.
He was quite ugly—small, with a large head and pop-eyes, and
frightfully arrogant. And he was simply devastating with women.
I could quite see it, too. But I never slept with him. He asked me
once, and he said he'd never ask me again, and I didn't and he
didn't."

"I never thought you did," said Gordon.

"Didn't you?" I said. "You should have seen him. I often
wondered why he had this tremendous attraction for women. I
think it was with him the way Goethe says it in that poem, *komm
den Frauen ʒart entgegen:* If you are tender with women, you
might get them; if you are bold, you'll do even better; but if you
insult them by your indifference then you are the real seducer."

"That's all very well," said Gordon, "but you've only dragged
in Dent to get away from your red shoes."

"You are really like that, too, I mean, indifferent and insulting," I said.

"And on top of it I'm older than young Dent," said Gordon,
"but not as old as Goethe in his prime, when he was at the height
of his fame. I'm still too young for you. What you really want is
the powerful old man. Now, tell me, what do these red shoes remind you of? I know we must keep on the straight and narrow
path with them. We must not get them messed up again. I wonder why?"

"You should know," I said, giving him a haughty look.

"Don't get distracted now," he said. "What do they make you think of?"

"Of the Andersen fairy-tale, of course," I said; "of the girl with the red shoes. She wants them so badly, and she is so vain she puts them on, on a Sunday to go to church, which is most improper and sinful, and in church she starts to dance and can't stop herself, and dances out of the church and she can't get rid of them, and she dances on and on till she falls dead. I suppose Cobbie was right and the shoes are a bit tarty. Apart from being non-regulation with uniform, of course. Do you know, about this going on and on and not being able to stop, I sometimes dream I'm in a red sports car, bright red, just like my shoes, and I'm driving it and it goes downhill, on and on, and I can't brake, and it goes on, but the smash doesn't come, so it's not the same as in the fairy-tale. The car just comes to a stop on its own. I suppose, really, red is a sort of sinful, non-regulation colour. And—"

I fell silent. I had wanted to tell Gordon how Cobbie, when she was drunk, used to go to the men's lavatory, but I had decided against it.

"Why did you stop all of a sudden?" asked Gordon. "You were associating so nicely."

"What's that?" I asked. "I was just talking."

"So you were," said Gordon; "but why did you stop?"

"I've no idea," I said crossly.

"Haven't you?" he asked, watching me with that look.

For a while we continued in silence.

Then I said, "Talking of cars, my husband had three cars, but two of them he couldn't use because of petrol rationing, but every week-end, and even sometimes at night, he spent hours cleaning them and taking them to bits and putting them together again, quite senseless. Why did he do it? Were the cars like women to him? Was it a sort of love-making, or what? And lots of his friends did the same, too."

"It's very common," remarked Gordon, "but it's quite the contrary of what you think. The cars are extensions of his own personality, and the more powerful they are, the more powerful he thinks he is."

"That's very interesting," I exclaimed.

"But you don't really care," said Gordon; "you've offered me this as a sop because you've stopped yourself talking. But I promise you, my poor child, I'll get there just the same. I've got there already, as it is."

Chapter

Fifteen

It was about a month after our walk in Regent's Park, when I had worn my red shoes for the first time again, that we were sitting in Gordon's room and I was telling him more of young Dent's stories, which, though not typical of Dent's nature, were yet peculiar to him, insofar as they would happen only to him and not to anyone else in our crowd.

"An Oxford don, a colonel, surnamed 'Fine Arts and Monuments' because his job was to see about the repatriation of the stolen pictures in Germany, was assigned to our mess. On his first morning, Fine Arts and Monuments comes down to breakfast, looks round for an empty chair and goes to Dent's table. Dent rises and says, 'Good morning, sir,' and Fine Arts and Monuments says, 'May I join you? By the way, I'm homosexual, do you mind?' Of course, Dent made the most of it. He dined out on it for weeks," and I burst into laughter.

Gordon remained unmoved. "Not bad," he said, "but why do you think it's so funny? After all, you've had a homosexual experience yourself."

"How dare you," I said, flaring up; "I'm not a lesbian."

"Why are you so upset?" said Gordon. "You had a try at it, though, didn't you? With the welfare officer. You told me in so many words. It happened after that scene with the red shoes. Definitely. You did it mainly out of vanity, because you were flattered by her. And you got a kick out of it because it was sinful and non-regulation. But you didn't enjoy it. You don't want to be messed up again on the soggy ground, you want to keep walking on the proper paths. Afterwards, you consoled yourself with the thought that there would be no smash-up, at least. Whatever she'd done, she couldn't make you pregnant."

"You are beastly," I said.

"Beastly but right," said Gordon; "and she did go on and on and on?"

"Yes, she did," I said, "about ten times. I don't know how she did it."

One evening the women's welfare officer joined the table in the ante-room where I was sitting. She had been to a party given by other-ranks girls in their mess; they were young women mainly employed as typists and clerks.

"I need a drink," she roared, "after sitting face-to-face with these floozies for hours on end."

After having finished her gin-and-water in moody silence, she turned to me, murmuring, "Come upstairs with me. *On va faire des bêtises ce soir.*" And she left soon, saying, "I'm off now, children. I can't stand the sight of your bloody faces any more."

The *"bêtises"* turned out to be most disappointing, with Cobbie lying on top of me and rubbing herself against my thigh; she kept her eyes open and I could see each time how they filmed over. In between she kept telling me that she should not be doing this, because "her ticker wasn't up to it," and that it was all my fault because I was "simply delicious."

I could not return her compliment. Cobbie was no more than an imitation of the crusty old general whom Gordon liked to act in public in order to embarrass me, and just as Gordon had guessed, I consoled myself with the thought that at least it was safe.

I still did not know what "associating" was; but I felt that my ignorance was similar to that in *Le Bourgeois Gentilhomme* when the parvenu learns to his astonishment that all his life he has been speaking prose.

"Cobbie left the army, too." I said. "I met her on a bus the other day. She looks just the same as she did in uniform; she still wears a collar and tie. She's a warden in a hostel now, for university women. That should suit her. She never could stand floozies."

"Not thrilling," said Gordon.

"I can't understand you," I said; "whenever I find somebody interesting, you are bored. And when I drivel at random, you are interested. We really have nothing in common."

"We'll go out now," said Gordon. "I'm meeting the commissioner of lunacy for a drink. But without the wife. She's doing her Christmas shopping."

"Where will he be?" I asked.

"In a pub behind Selfridges," he said.

As we were crossing Wigmore Street, I said, still stung by his refusal to be interested in Cobbie, "That commissioner of yours is so dull except for his title." And as he did not reply, I added, "Why don't you let me meet Dr. Bruce? He sounds much more fun."

"He's dead," said Gordon, "didn't you know? No, of course not, you don't read the papers. He did himself in."

"Really? Why?" I asked.

"Who knows?" said Gordon.

When we got to the bar where the commissioner was already waiting for us, I did not get any elucidation, either, though they discussed Bruce's suicide at length; I could not make any sense of it, all the more so as I had come to realise by then that such terms as "depression" and "hysteria" did not mean what I thought they did and referred to states of mind about which I knew nothing at all. I gave up listening.

It reminded me of what my friend Monica's husband had told me recently, when I went to see her. He was a biologist and had gone to a lecture at the Royal Society given by a biologist from America. "The only thing I understood," he said, "was, refreshments will be served at four-thirty."

Monica was the only one of my women friends whom I had carried over from my teens. I had lost touch with her during the war and had found her again, living in London, and married, when I had returned from Germany.

Now, after we had parted from the commissioner and were walking towards Oxford Street, I said to Gordon: "You know, all your talk just now was for me exactly the way Monica's husband put it the other day," and I told him about it.

"Ah, yes," he said, "my poor child. You were rather left out in the cold, weren't you?"

"Not really," I said. "I never feel left out in the cold when I'm with you."

"That's because I'm so kind to you," he remarked, leering at me, "just like a kind father."

"Oh, stop it now," I said; "don't get on to that again. Anyway, my father wasn't kind, ever; I've just remembered something about him from the old days when I was small and we were living in Vienna."

"Tell me," he said.

"I came into the drawing room," I said; "I know exactly how it was furnished, too, with a wallpaper of yellow brocade. I remember the whole flat, anyway. He'd just come home. And I ran up to him and took his hand. And I got burned. He was holding his cigarette like this—with his hand down his side, you see, and with the back of the hand showing and the cigarette between his fingers, inside the hand, so that it was hidden. I couldn't have possibly known it was there. So there you are, I want to greet him and he burns me."

"It's not true," said Gordon; "you made it up."

"But I didn't," I exclaimed. "I can still see the blister I had there, on this finger."

"No," said Gordon, "you've made it up. You've probably dreamt it and it stuck in your mind."

"But how can you tell?" I asked.

"Never mind. I just can," he said; "and you don't remember anything about your father. Perhaps one day I'll make you. But it doesn't suit me just now."

I moved my shoulders to dispel the shiver of apprehension which passed through me; and as he remained silent, I started to tell him about Monica, because it was the first thing that came to my mind.

"I like her a lot," I said, "but I always feel guilty when I see her. She doesn't know anything about it, but I feel guilty just the same."

"Go on," he said. "We'll eat in Edgware Road. This will keep me happy till we get there."

I had met Monica when I was eighteen and she a year older. She had come to my home town to study at the university, and all the people who met her went out of their way to make her welcome, though this had nothing to do with her own merits, those of a handsome, modest, and clever young girl. Her father was one of the richest men in the country. I had known Monica for about a half a year when she asked me to a tea-party at her little flat.

When I got there, I found the living room filled with something like fifteen young men, undergraduates by the looks of them, all of whom, I decided after a quick glance, were unattractive. They were seated in such a way as to form an oval, and at the far end of the room stood a much older man, lounging against the wall, with his hands in his pockets, making a speech.

I caught something about "custom barriers and *laisser-faire*." He looked at me as I entered and continued to speak. I had clearly burst into the middle of a lecture.

Monica motioned me to a chair which stood near the door and whispered into my ear, "I had to get them for him. He just loves to air his pet theories. He's only here for a two-day visit."

"Who is he?" I murmured.

"My father," she replied.

"But he doesn't look like you," I whispered.

"I take after my mother," she said.

I settled down and tried to listen. It was like going to sleep in a railway carriage, with states of alertness getting submerged by states of slumber.

He did not look rich at all. He had a narrow, thin-lipped, clever, hungry face, with dark, hungry, burning eyes, and dark greying hair which lay in untidy waves round his forehead. He was negligently dressed in creased old tweeds. When he stopped speaking, I saw Monica leaving the room, by the other door, followed by two young men, laughing and joking; she was obviously getting tea ready. Then I saw her father coming towards me. I felt uneasy, wondering if I had been able to conceal the boredom I had been subjected to, and hoped he would not ask me how I had enjoyed the lecture.

He stopped by my chair with his eyes fastened on me. I decided it would be silly to smile in the face of economics; I met his eyes gravely.

"Will you come with me to the cinema tonight?" he asked.

"Yes," I said.

"Meet me at the Élysée at nine," he said, turned, and left me. We did not exchange another word that afternoon.

When we met in the evening, we were shown to a box. The film had already started. I was watching the screen and he was watching me. Once he raised his hand from the red plush ledge and moved his fingers over my breasts. I remained quite still, but I was burning with mortification; the reason for this was that I was wearing a bust bodice of lace, strengthened at the lower rim by a wire covered in pink velvet. Up till now I had been greatly impressed by this garment and wore it on special occasions only; but as his fingers moved over me and touched the hard wire, I imagined he must be convinced I was wearing an artificial bosom. When he withdrew his hand, I said to myself, And no wonder. That's enough to put a man off for good.

After the cinema he slowly walked me home in the mild April night. I was silent and still furious about my wired bodice, while he told me an incident of his boyhood.

"There were several dishes which were my favourites," he said, "and whenever my mother was pleased with me, she would cook one of them."

God, how ghastly, I thought, the mother did the cooking herself. I was surprised they were that poor.

He went on, "Then, one day, when this happened again, and my mother asked me which of my favourites I would like, I said, 'That lovely pancake which you made last time for me.' 'But you had it last time,' she said, and I said, 'Yes, I know, but I only want the pancake again.' And after this it was the pancake again and the pancake for ever after. You see, for the first time in my life I had discovered the nature of love. When it's love, you want the one thing and the one thing only."

"I suppose so," I remarked, feeling his eyes on me, while

thinking that never again would I wear that blasted bra. This was just his polite way of telling me he cared for someone else.

He said, "I'll be staying here for another two days and then I'll be going for three weeks to Bellagio. This is the best time of the year for the lakes. Will you come with me?"

"I can't," I said; "my mother'd never let me."

I did not know whether he was aware of the genuine regret I felt.

"So you see," I concluded, "I'd have gone with him like a shot. And Monica has no idea about it."

"But tell me," said Gordon, "what made you so keen? Because he was so rich?"

"Don't be so idiotic," I said; "I didn't want to get anything out of him. He was the sort of man who can make and un-make cabinet ministers and get politics changed, but I don't care for politics, either; that's why I don't read the paper. Can't you understand? He was outstanding, altogether. All the years I knew Monica she was moaning and groaning how insipid every man was compared to her father. Nobody she ever met could hold a candle to him. I shut up, of course; I didn't want her to know."

"I see," said Gordon, "and what kind of man did she marry?"

"Oh, he's quite distinguished, too, really," I said; "a scientist. Frightfully old, though. Thirty years older than she is."

"You amaze me," said Gordon. "Who would have thought it? You should have done the same, don't you think?"

"Marry a man as old as that? I'm not crazy," I said.

"You must forgive me for being so dense," said Gordon, "but you never did like young men, did you?"

"Not really," I said, "no, never. I suppose I'm just made that way."

"And you'd better stay that way," said Gordon. "I know when I'm well off."

That night, when we were in his room, Gordon indulged in one of those jokes of his which annoyed me. He put a cigarette in a holder which he rarely used, lit it as he came to the bed and placed it on the ashtray on the bedside table. As soon as he had entered me, he seized the holder and started to smoke, while continuing to use me, which he did with feeble, lackadaisical movements.

I got angry and yelled that he should stop.

He went on smoking, with gestures of finicky dandified elegance and affectation, which increased my anger, till, after two minutes of toying with me and the cigarette, he alternately abandoned it and availed himself of my body with the grave, bitter concentration I knew so well. I closed my eyes with relief and surrendered to his invasion, which was relentless, ever returning, like the sea beating against the shore.

When I came home on the following morning, I was met by Mr. Sewell in the hall.

As soon as he caught sight of me, he clutched his head in his hands. "You people——" He started.

"Yes, I know," I said, "we expect the Ritz, and look at the rents we pay."

"You should be paying double," he said, "when you think what I do for you."

"Since when?" I asked. "Last time you said——"

"I know. But this time I've saved your bacon for you," he remarked.

"That's not much," I said, moving towards the stairs, "the ration being what it is. And now I'm dying for my breakfast and bath."

"You'll soon be in more hot water than is good for you," he remarked, rolling his eyes in an ominous fashion.

"Why?" I asked.

"Do you know who phoned today?" he said, putting one foot on the first step of stairs and placing one hand on his hip while resting the other on the newel post. Observing his monumental attitude, I resigned myself to having to endure him for a few more minutes.

"Who phoned?" I asked.

"Mr. Walbrook. Ever heard of the gent before?" he said.

"Mmm," I said. "I didn't know he was in London. I thought he was in New Zealand. Or in Leicester."

"He's here now," said Mr. Sewell, "rings up in the morning, with the dew still on him, at half past eight, and wants to speak to you. And where are you? You're on the tiles, on the beat, wearing a nightie with a hem of fur because you want to keep your neck warm."

"Oh, God," I said.

"And I couldn't even tell him you'd gone round to shop at Whiteleys," said Mr. Sewell, "because they don't open before nine."

"What did you say?" I asked. What if my husband were to find out that Gordon was my lover, and then made trouble for Gordon? But Gordon, I decided, could take care of himself. He could make rings round my husband, I thought, contemptuously.

"What did you say?" I repeated.

"That you'd gone off to the country with your friend Monica," said Mr. Sewell, "near Maidenhead—that was a good one, wasn't it? And that I didn't have your phone number there, and that you'd be back sometime today. You better go and ring him up, now. Bend the knee and bow the head. You getting a divorce for desertion, aren't you, lucky girl? Don't want to mess up things in the last minute."

"Where is he staying?" I asked.

"He's staying at the Ritz, but the number is in the phone book under Strand Palace Hotel."

"He would," I said.

"Get on with it," said Mr. Sewell. "Room four-one-four. Here are the pennies. No excuses."

"Thank you very much," I said.

"Be pleasant," he said; "it costs the same money. I'll leave you now, draw the veil of decency and all that," and he abandoned his posture and disappeared into his private office on the ground floor.

Chapter

Sixteen

The day after Gordon left to spend the Christmas week with one of his married sisters in Scotland, I received a letter from friends in Leicester, with which they had enclosed a cutting from the *Leicester Herald*. It was in the tiny print which is used for unimportant local news, and the full name of the court, the judge, and the firm of solicitors occupied more space than the statement of the divorce itself.

Gordon returned in the New Year. He rang me up at his usual hour, at ten in the morning, and told me to come to his place at six in the afternoon.

During his absence I had not been unhappy. Being invited to other people's houses had given me a feeling of superiority, as I compared their insipidly pleasant state to my own. There was a barrier between them and me, invisible but impassable, like the invisible bars in modern zoos, where the tropical animals are confined within their ground by a space of heated air.

At the same time, I knew that they in turn would have been uncomprehending if they had known that my contentment came from a man who was able to say, "I shall hold you for ever, because I shall always find new ways of torturing you," and that my own particular paradise of the green fitted carpet, the blond machine-carved furniture, and the pressed-glass vases was paradise only because I did not dwell there of my own free will but was held in bondage there.

On this afternoon, however, I did not even get within sight of the pressed-glass vases, because, as soon as Gordon closed the door behind me, he lifted me up, laid me on the hall floor and took possession of me there.

"This is such a dull place. If at least it were sordid," I remarked as we sat down to dinner, "but no. It's revoltingly clean and bright. I'm sure it's run by Swiss." He had taken me to a restaurant in Baker Street where we had never been before.

"I'm very dull myself," he said; "it's the backwash from having been home. It was deadly in Scotland. What people call having a good rest. Three times they dragged me to the theatre—that was most restful, too. I can't stand the theatre. It's as much as I can do not to fall asleep."

"I can't understand you," I said. "I love the theatre."

"Whatever they've got on the stage," he said, "it's nothing to what my patients tell me."

"You are being ridiculous," I said. "Your patients, that's life. And the theatre is art. If somebody gets run over by a car, that's very sad, but it's not the stuff for a play. But if somebody knew the car was coming, and still walked into it and got killed, then that would be tragedy in the Greek way. That would be art."

"It would be life, too, my poor child," said Gordon; "and I wish they wouldn't give chips with everything."

"I could have told you they would as soon as I saw the place," I said, "but you have no feeling for atmosphere."

"Oh, dear, oh, dear, now you want to punish me again," he said in a voice quavering with emotion, and bent his head. "Why am I always so unlucky with women?"

I laughed.

That night, when I was in bed, exhausted, Gordon, clad in his dragon-strewn dressing gown, was sitting at his desk and smoking. He looked, I thought resentfully, as smooth and unconcerned and invulnerable as the black cat when it had come sliding through the shattered pane in Mr. Sewell's kitchen and had partaken of the sardines laced with Worcestershire sauce.

"We'll go to bed now," he said; "it's time you went to sleep."

I got on to my knees and picked up the pillows which had been pushed aside and had fallen on the floor, because Gordon, in his desire to have me spread out flat, never allowed my head to rest on the pillows; when he wanted to go to sleep, I always arranged them for him.

I saw him walk to the cupboard and open one of its four little doors. When he turned round and came towards me, I sat on my heels, petrified, and only gave a scream as he was standing right in front of me.

He had been walking up to me, smiling, with a pair of large scissors raised in both hands, and as I screamed he snapped them shut within half an inch of my face.

"What are you so frightened of?" he asked, smiling with deep amusement.

"Put them away," I said.

He returned the scissors to the cupboard and came and sat on the edge of the bed.

"What did you think I'd do to you?" he asked.

"I thought you'd cut off my breasts," I said.

"That's quite normal," he said; "all your old fears are rising to the surface now. I've got a patient who starts up every time I click my lighter for a cigarette. He thinks I'm going to castrate him."

"I never jump at your lighter," I said; "don't be so idiotic."

"Of course you don't," he said; "you are fairly normal, after all. I just wanted to see. You are putting all your fears on to me now, all that you don't want. Like you put that piece of cheese on my plate, the other night, in Soho."

"I don't understand you," I said. "What old fears?"

He did not reply. He rose and laid his dressing gown on a chair.

"Make room for me," he said.

I smoothed the pillows, piled them up, and he stretched out on his back.

"Do you remember," he said, "that day when we had drinks with the commissioner and then walked up Oxford Street, and you told me about Monica's father?"

"Yes," I said.

"All the way to Marble Arch you took my hand and held it," he said.

"Did I? Yes, I did, I suppose," I said.

"Why did you?" he asked.

"Because Oxford Street is always so crowded," I said.

"Rubbish," said Gordon, "not at this time of night. You kept hold of my hand because you wanted protection. You wouldn't have done this a few months ago. It was a gesture of confidence."

I did not reply.

He said, "You are like every other woman. You want to be loved and protected." His voice had been derisive while saying this. I felt chilled and bewildered. I wondered to myself what was so bad about it. It was true. But why was it wrong?

"You are completely dependent on me," he said, "for your fears and for support." He closed his eyes. "I must get back into analysis," he added, while I, sitting on my heels, looked down at his unmoved face, searching in vain to grasp why I displeased him.

He said, "Come to me now, and go to sleep."

And while I draped my body across his and laid my head on his uncomfortable chest, he remained still, with his arms by his sides, and I wondered if ever the time would come when he would fold them round me.

Chapter

Seventeen

It was about a week later. We had been out to dinner and returned to Portman Square.

"Get undressed and go to bed," said Gordon as soon as we came in, and when he saw that I sat down on the settee and was rummaging in my handbag, he added, "Get your clothes off before I tear them off."

I undressed, took my handbag with me and sat down on the edge of the bed. I had dropped my bag in the street as we had crossed into Portman Square and the contents were tumbled about inside.

I continued putting my belongings into order, searching for my pocket comb and finding it had slid between the pages of my little notebook, slipping my tortoiseshell powder case into its leather sheath and disentangling my bunch of keys from a cluster of safety-pins.

I looked up briefly as Gordon entered, naked, from the hall.

"Lie down on the bed," he said.

I continued with my sorting out and saw with a sideways glance that he was moving to the cupboard. I gave my attention to my task till a sudden double-take made me glance up once more.

I had never looked inside his cupboard. I only knew that it was from there that he had produced the tin with the biscuits and, much more recently, the pair of scissors. God, not that again, I said to myself, and, placing the bag on the bedside table, I watched Gordon taking out of the cupboard something which I could not see. His back obscured my view.

He turned and came towards the bed with his arms behind him.

He was not smiling as he had done a week ago when brandishing the scissors. His face was unmoved.

An instant later he stood in front of me and my fear arose as I looked searchingly into his face, into his unevenly placed eyes with the white rings round the irises.

Then his face was hidden from my sight as he bent his head over me and suddenly lifted me up and I found myself lying face downwards, across him and on the bed, with him sitting and holding my legs tightly wedged between his knees and keeping me down with an arm pressing between my shoulders so that I was prostrated helplessly in his grasp. I twisted my head round, stunned, just as he gave me the first blow with the hammer he used for testing reflexes. It was white with a black handle, I could see, and I also could see his profile.

It bore that air of grave, unflinching concentration which I knew so well from his love-making.

I squealed as he struck me for the second time, and then I heard myself shrieking as I had never done before, with my nails convulsively clawing and releasing the edge of the mattress, while he kept beating me unmercifully with the slow, steady, relentless rhythm which was the same as when he was taking possession of me; and as my shrieks grew worse, he shifted his arm which lay across my shoulders and buried his hand in the nape of my neck and forced my head down and held my face crushed against the bed, half choking my cries.

He went on and on, so long and so hard and so steadily that I lost all sense of time, till, at one blow, I heard a sharp cracking sound like the click when an electric switch is turned off; his hand released my neck and, slightly raising my head from the sheet, I saw a white cylinder rolling on the floor, away from the bed and towards the settee.

It was only then that I realised that he had broken the hammer on my back.

He opened his knees and I dropped on to the floor and tumbled over, still too numbed to control my limbs.

For an instant I saw him sitting on the bed, his head lowered.

The next, he threw the black shaft away and was kneeling above me. He flung me on my back and, though I did not resist him, took possession of me, using me fiercely and desperately and frantically and with a burning defiance, as though rebelling against an invisible onlooker who was commanding him to stop.

When he gained the release from his rage and achieved his victory of rebellion and laid his head on my shoulder, I knew that I had stilled a fire which he had never appeased before, that he had wanted to do this to me from the first moment he had set eyes on me, and that all he had made me suffer up till then had only been in the nature of makeshifts and stopgaps to contain his desire.

I recalled his melancholy utterance about his winter coat: "The last one was good for six years. Now I've got this one. And after this there'll be one more—maybe." But there were to be no other women for him. He had done to me what he had never done to anyone else before and what he would do to no one else after me. I was the only woman for him, made to measure.

But I was too well tailored for his needs. I fitted him too perfectly. I knew that it would not be long before he dragged me from the rim of darkness into the centre of it, and what would wait for me there I did not know. Or, to be more truthful, I did not want to know.

I was as bad as he was, and he knew it. I had obeyed him and submitted to him from the beginning, and upon my remark

"If someone knew the car was coming, and still walked into it, and got killed, that would be art," he had replied, "It would be life, too."

I felt light and clean and weak, and I felt light and free in my heart, too, absolved from all responsibility and anxiety over making decisions; the car which had been set in motion on that afternoon at Shepherds when I had risen from the windowsill was gaining speed now and had just come into view.

"Come on, get up," he said, and as I sat up he put his hands under my armpits and lifted me on to the bed.

While I had been in surrender to him, on the floor, I had not been in pain. Now as I touched the sheet I felt as though he had laid me on a bunch of heated knives.

"Oh," I exclaimed, catching my breath.

"Turn over, then," he said, "and stay on your tummy."

"Give me a cigarette," I said, lying down carefully on my side and raising myself on one elbow.

While he went over to the desk to fetch his case, I looked at the floor. The top part of the hammer was gone and so was the handle.

He returned and watched me while lighting my cigarette. My hand was trembling slightly.

"Lie down," he said, "and I'll undo your hair."

"But then I can't smoke," I said.

"Don't smoke then," he replied.

"But I've only just lit it," I said.

"Don't annoy me," he said, and he took it from my hand and laid it on the ashtray, next to my handbag. I lay down properly and watched it smouldering while he opened my hair. "Trust you to put your bag in the only place where it is in the way," he said in the fretful, whining cockney voice; "you are dreadful, you women."

Wondering what pretext he would have used for punishing me if it had not been for the offending object, I said hastily, "I'll have to get a new one for my new suit. It should be ready the beginning of next month. And I'd like to have a pink blouse to go with it, and pink shoes. Or perhaps not. Perhaps that would be too tarty."

"I don't know what you have against tarts," he remarked; "a perfectly good profession spoilt by amateurs."

I laughed, rolling over. "Oh, God," I exclaimed, turning back on my side.

He watched me quite unmoved.

"I'd like to kill you," I said.

"That's nothing new," he remarked.

We continued in silence for a long time.

I watched him smoking. I did not ask him for another cigarette. It was only when he joined me in bed and I was about to settle down for sleep that I asked, humbly and faintly, "Why did you do it?"

He said, "Because you needed it, my sweet child."

I dug my chin into his chest and raised my glance and I saw his lids closing more tightly over his shut eyes.

When I saw him again on the following evening, he watched me undressing, but he did not ask me if I still was in pain; and though I felt furious with him at this way of making me suffer and withholding all consolation, I lay down for him submissively spread out the way he liked it, and waited, trembling with longing until he took me.

Chapter

Eighteen

On the day when I had the first fitting for my suit at the tailor's, I went to Portman Square at six in the afternoon.

As Gordon opened the door to me, I could hear that the wireless was on and music was coming from his room, and he told me in a low voice to sit down for a while, as he wanted to listen.

He had never done this before. He knew that to me modern music was unenjoyable, and he always turned off the wireless when I was with him in his room; he always gave me his full attention—whether pleasantly or hurtfully was beside the point.

I sat down on the settee.

After ten minutes he switched it off and said, "Is it still raining?"

"No," I said, "only wet underfoot."

"I don't feel like going out just now," he said; "undress and lie down."

I undressed.

I was angry because he had hardly spoken a word to me, and when he came over to the bed, I curled up and struggled as he shifted me, and then, when I was on my back, I made difficulties again and would not let him come between my thighs.

He dealt with me as usual, silent and unmoved, and made me cry out as he entered me, and as he went on, he penetrated me painfully with his slow, avid, insatiable determination till my resistance was broken and he received from me the helpless surrender he always achieved.

He got up at once after he had reached his satisfaction, went over to the wireless, switched it on, tried several stations and turned it off.

"Get dressed now," he said without turning round, "and I'll get dressed, too."

I thought, Why does he say it in this way? Of course he'll get dressed, too. He's not going to the pub naked.

I forced myself to get up. I was still weak. He always used to consider me, and gave me time for rest, and this was the first time he had not done so.

I was ready sooner than he.

He was sitting on the settee in his shirtsleeves, without his tie and without his shoes, looking into space.

I sat down behind the desk when I saw him get up and cross over to the cupboard, to that Pandora's box of the four doors, to that bastard piece of blond wood on bow-legs, crested by the shop-soiled fancy of wholesale furniture makers with a carved spray of roses and knotted ribbon.

He was approaching the cupboard, tiptoeing up to it, with the stealth of a ham actor who by his exaggerated secretiveness draws the attention of the whole audience. Still acting, he turned his head to see if he were safe from spying eyes. He opened one of the doors and looked over his shoulder, leering at me conspiratorially with one of his crocodile grins.

He said, "You see, I've got my rations. One egg, butter, and bacon. I'm going to have them cooked for me."

And though, from where I was sitting, I could not see the contents of the cupboard, he hastily slammed the door shut, as though unwilling to let me spy out his secret.

He returned to the settee and undid the laces of one shoe.

I said, "You've got another woman, haven't you?"

"How do you know?" he asked, and when I did not speak, he added, "Of course you know. One always knows. She's seventeen years old and I'll be sick and tired of her in a fortnight. But that's got nothing to do with it. That's neither here nor there."

I felt no stab of jealousy. The only one I had been jealous of was Gordon's former wife, and even she had evaporated from the jealousy-compartment of my heart. I had known for a long time now that all he had made me submit to he had never demanded from anyone else, and that the tortures he had lavished on me raised me to a value no other woman could have.

I remained silent.

"It's got to stop," he said, slipping into his shoe and lacing it. "I shan't see you any more. I'll take you home now. I've got a splitting headache."

I still did not speak.

"It can't go on like this," he said; "you've become completely dependent on me. You can't take a step without me any more."

I considered this for a while. He was right, of course, even in the crudest sense. I did not even get dressed or undressed unless he told me to, and I did not dare as much as to wash my hands or smoke a cigarette without his permission.

"It's true," I said, "but that's been going on for ages. Why bring it up now? You want to be rid of me, and that's all there is to it."

"I don't want to be rid of you," he said; "I've got to. It's come to a point where it's got to stop. Besides, I'm going back into analysis now. I can't do it with you. You'd be in my way. So that's that."

He was fully shod by now, but he remained seated, his head bowed, looking down at his feet.

I said in a low, calm, even voice, "You've hurt me terribly. I'll never get over it."

"Fiddlesticks!" he exclaimed with heavily acted joviality. "Of course you'll get over it. Don't talk rubbish."

I did not speak.

He grew serious and looked at me, longingly and searchingly.

He said, "Sexually, I'd never tire of you. I could go on with you for ever," and when I remained silent, he added, "But it's got to stop. You want from me what everybody wants from a father. You want punishment and protection. You've made me into a complete father-figure."

I grew angry. He had thrown me out, I did not know why; it was a stroke of lightning, an earthquake, a tidal wave; it was something to be taken without query and without redress.

But now, to cover up, he played the professional mind-reader, the juggler of souls, the conjurer of emotions, the magician who called up and dissolved images at will; he had to perform, he was giving the sack to his girl, and still he had to whisk his particular white rabbit out of his particular top hat, had to use his jargon and his skill.

"Father-figure," I said. "Of course. Father-figure. I've been waiting for this. First it was Derek O'Teague and now it's you. It's part of your stock-in-trade."

He said, "Derek O'Teague was a pale shadow. He didn't have a chance against me. To me you sold yourself body and soul."

Yes, it's true, I thought. Again, to put it at its crudest, who but one's own father would tell one when to go to the lavatory, and who but a daughter would obey? Who but one's own father would put you over his knee and give you a thorough beating?

"Tell me," he said.

"You are right," I remarked; "it's never occurred to me before. But it's true. You are—you were—like a father to me."

"Of course I'm right," he said, and added with exaggerated

GORDON

heartiness, "Like a kind father. Anyway, what are you complaining about? You've had three hundred guineas' worth of treatment as it is."

I looked at him aghast.

He said, "Of course. What do you think it was? Let's go now," and he slipped into his coat. "When you get over it," he added, "you'll ring me up and we'll meet and have a real pow-wow," still keeping his tone of false heartiness.

I did not reply.

We went out in silence and walked in silence along Oxford Street and continued in silence towards Marble Arch. It was cold and drizzling.

Pow-wow, I thought, we'll have a pow-wow. He would use this word. Now. He's never used it before. Pow-wow is what the Red Indians have. A get-together. He is so jolly and so false he cannot trust himself to speak decent honest-to-God English. Not with me. Not any more. Not with me any more. Sexually he'd never tire of me, that's why it's got to stop. He could go on with me for ever. That's why it's got to stop. He doesn't want to get rid of me; that's why he's got to get rid of me. Nothing but disguise. And he retreats behind his father-figure. Why don't I make a scene? Why am I so well behaved? I am a lady, just the way my mother said it: "A lady is a woman who behaves well in any situation and can help herself in none."

Gordon stopped in front of the Marble Arch underground station. "I shan't see you home," he said. "I've got this splitting headache. And don't forget, when you are over it, ring me up."

"I shan't ring you up," I said, "unless it's something special."

"Don't say 'special,' say 'especial,'" he said.

"Yes," I said.

193

"You'd better take the tube," he remarked; "you shouldn't stand about in this weather."

If given the choice of public transport, I would have preferred the bus despite the drizzle. But I was obedient to the last.

"Yes, I'll take the tube," I said. I turned away and entered the underground station.

Chapter

Nineteen

It was in the late afternoon, towards the end of January. I was sitting in the drawing room, dressed to go out for dinner, waiting for my husband.

I'm glad it's getting late, I kept telling myself, the later the better. If I say it now, when he's in a hurry, it'll be easier. There'll be no time to thrash it out.

My husband came in.

"I'm ready now," he said. "I thought he'd never stop talking. Even told me the weather they've been having in London, at the rate of three pounds per three minutes. Thank God it wasn't my call."

"Who was it?" I asked. "That man from Sotheby's?"

"Yes," he said, "writing hasn't yet been invented for him. I always said he was illiterate. He gets his stuff by sticking pins into catalogues. Shall we go now?"

"Yes," I said, "and by the way—"

I used the "by the way" which is an expression introducing a subject of slight importance, and yet, what I was going to say was of the greatest importance to me. Of such a desperate importance that I was willing to risk the break-up of my marriage and all the security that went with it.

"And by the way," I was saying, "I wanted to tell you—I must go to London."

"Why?" asked my husband.

"I just must go," I said.

"But why?" he asked. "What's your reason?"

I remained silent.

"For what purpose?" he asked.

"I want to get away from things," I said.

"But why to London?" he asked. "Because I've just had a call from London? And if it had been from Rome, you'd say you must go to Rome? Or what?"

"I want to get away from the house and the domesticity," I said.

"All right," he said, "but if you want to get away, now, at this time of the year, from the Madrid winter, why don't you go to Malaga or the Canaries? You could go with Lady Ellis, she's going in a week or so. The Da Costas are going, too. Not he, of course, but the wife and the mother-in-law."

"No," I said, "I want to go to London."

"But why?" he asked.

"I want to look up my friends," I said, "and do some shopping."

"But you've just been," said my husband; "we've been in London—when was it? October, beginning of November. Three months ago. You had it all three months ago."

"I didn't have the chance to see anybody properly then," I said. "I had to trail round with you all the time."

"You must be mad," said my husband; "before this, you hadn't been to London for four years. And you never missed it."

"That's true," I said, "but now I've got to go."

"You're mad," said my husband. "Look here. It's late as it is. And you've got to spring this on me. Just now. First that long-distance call and now this. Like the boiler which always burns through on a Saturday night but never on a week-day. We'll discuss it later."

"There's nothing to discuss," I said, "and I do feel like the burnt-out boiler."

"You're mad," said my husband. "When you get to London, do me a favour, will you? Go to see a psychiatrist and just tell him you are mad."

"I will," I said.

"And tell the maid to leave the big lights on now," he said. "She forgot again last night."

"I will," I said, and followed him out into the hall.

I could not tell to what extent my husband realised that I was desperately set on going to London. But he must have realised some of my despair, because during the following days he merely asked me whether I was going to stay with my cousin Sylvia. I said I would not, because she had not enough room, and that I would book at a hotel.

Since my marriage some four years ago, I had not travelled anywhere on my own, and I had been prepared, in case my husband would not agree to my request, to sell my jewelry behind his back, so as to raise some money for the journey.

The heart beats all the time and one is not aware of it. It is only when one becomes aware of it that one complains of palpitations.

In the same way, I had been, up till now, carrying my grief for Gordon with a quiet and steady desolation; never a day passed without my being reminded of him, and taking it for granted.

Till suddenly, one morning, shortly after our return from London early in November, my grief broke into violence and my desolation into fury. I became aware that I could not go on living any more without getting the answer to my questions: Why did he throw me out? And why did he kill himself?

The night before, I had gone to the cinema with my husband

and seen a French film in which the main actor bore a resemblance to Gordon. Upon coming home, during the night, I had dreamt of him. I had never dreamt of him before, and what was worse, in the dream he had laid me on my back across his knees and had kissed me longingly and hotly on the lips, saying, "I'll take you home with me now. I'll keep you imprisoned for six weeks to start with, and I'll never let you go."

Whether my furious despair was set off by the image of Gordon, who had never before come to me in a dream, or whether it was that I had dreamt of receiving kisses from him, who had never kissed me when he was alive, I could not say.

In the course of one night the underground river had eroded the soil beneath which it had been flowing quietly and turbidly for the last eight years; it had welled over the banks and was flooding and swamping my life.

For three months I tried to fight the floods. I was still exasperated when I asked for a knife and the maid brought it in her hand instead of on a plate.

I was still amused when the gardener gave me a bunch of orchids as a Christmas present, which the Countess Almeida, coming to dinner, promptly recognised as having been stolen from the hot-houses of her friend Mrs. Warburton.

I still asked the cook if I should engage an extra maid for her, to close the doors behind her and to turn the lights out.

But I took no interest in these happenings any more, just as I was not able to read a single book and spent my time gazing somewhere above the printed page. Just as, when entertaining, I did not listen any more to the gossip of my guests and paid no attention to what was being said.

The ties of ordinary life were frayed and thinning day by day. The despair that raged within me was estranging me from the outside world. I began to understand the meaning of the word "alienated"; I was becoming an alien, a stranger, an outsider, and against my own will.

I realised that there was only one way for me to become appeased. The time had come to take the tin of corned beef out of the deep-freeze compartment. I had to go and see Dr. Crombie.

During the last eight years, since Gordon's death, Dr. Crombie's image had not changed, though he had grown in importance. I had acquired the habit, when going to a bookshop or library, to take from the shelves any book on psychiatry I happened to see, open it at the back, find the index, and search for the letter *C*. And Crombie, tall, beefy, short-necked, pug-nosed, mean-eyed, suspicious, vain, imperious, self-righteous, masterful, was always there. He was quoted in every work, English or American, flatteringly mostly, and sometimes derisively; but he was there. And reassured as to the prime quality of my tin of corned beef, my iron ration for an emergency, I restored the book to its place.

When my husband asked me, "For how long do you want to stay?" I said unhesitatingly, "For six weeks," and only realised after I had given the answer that those "six weeks" came out of my dream, from the words Gordon had spoken.

When my husband asked me, "Where do you want to stay?" I said, again unhesitatingly, "In the Belgrave Park Hotel," and again I realised only afterwards that this was because the Belgrave Park Hotel was still tied in my mind with deceit, faithlessness, double-crossing, and trying to leave one's husband.

That this time I had no intention of leaving my husband, and that I was not open to the chance of finding a lover, made no difference. I had the superstitious belief that things would only turn out well for me if I descended at the Belgrave Park Hotel.

Chapter

Twenty

When I arrived, the hotel looked the same; but once I entered the foyer, I did not recognise it. The Victorian gilt and blue plush, the bronze goddesses holding lamps and the tall spotted mirrors which had reflected them were gone. The high ceiling of scrolled stucco work had gone, too, and there was now a plain ceiling, lowered, depriving the place of its former spacious grandeur. I stood in a modern, insipidly furnished lounge, with imitation-leather seats and imitation-marble-topped tables. There was a special desk for booking theatre tickets and another for booking sightseeing tours, and illuminated arrows pointed the way to the buttery, the grill-room, and the restaurant.

I had arrived on a Wednesday evening. On Thursday morning I rang up Dr. Crombie; he was still at the same address in Harley Street where he had been in Gordon's time. How often and how longingly had I looked it up, tempted by the thought of seeing him, picturing to myself what dress I was going to wear, and never daring to.

What if he won't see me? I thought. He's the king of the Bloomsbury Clinic, he's mentioned in every book, he hasn't been waiting for me. He'll be booked up for months ahead. Or what if he sees me and throws me out? Or what if he'll only see me if I bring a letter from my own doctor?

An elderly woman's voice answered the call.

"You can't speak to Dr. Crombie," she said.

"Can you make an appointment for me?" I asked.

"No, I can't do that," she said; "but ring here again tomorrow, between eleven and twelve. What was the name again?"

When I rang off, I thought, I'll never get through to him at all.

I rang up the following morning at half past eleven and the elderly voice answered again.

"The doctor will see you on Monday," she said, "at twelve o'clock, mid-day."

I spent the following three days in a torment of doubt and fear and anxiety, which was only stilled when I was shown into the waiting room on Monday.

It was then, to my amusement, that I recognised Crombie's dining room, which I had pictured in my mind's eye; my phantasy had not been very daring—I had simply made use of the standard waiting room, prevalent up and down Harley Street, with the large mahogany board and the imitation-Chippendale chairs.

I now had on what I had never seen in my fancies when dreaming of this occasion; I was wearing a plain dark green wool dress and a mink coat. When my name was called, I took off the fur and draped it negligently over my arm, recalling a saying of my mother's: "If you can't wear a mink coat like a piece of sacking, you are not fit to have one."

The attendant led me to a lift and we got out on the second floor; we walked down an exceedingly long passage and she opened a door at its end and held it open for me. I stepped inside and heard the click as she shut the door behind my back.

I remained where I was, looking at Dr. Crombie.

He was standing by a small round table halfway across the large room; he put down a book as I came in. He was not at all as I had imagined him and yet, now that I saw him, I could not believe that I had ever thought he might look different from what he was. He was a fairly tall and very powerfully built old man, with strong, wide shoulders and a massive chest. His white hair, thin in the middle, was full and fluffy at the sides of his round, pale face. He had a straight, short nose with violet veins on it, his mouth was round and firmly closed like an oyster, and he looked at me over the rim of his glasses, unsmiling, but with a faintly jolly, expectant air.

With his old-fashioned black coat, grey waistcoat and striped trousers, and a gold watch-chain glinting aslant his waist, he was the image of the consultant physician of my childhood; he was the picture of what servants like to call "such a kind, dear old gentleman." Yet I did not think he was kind.

My main impression was that of power, and his mild, calm air made me think of those famous opera stars who manage to breathe a *pianissimo*, barely audible trill and yet make one feel that the potential hidden strength and volume of their voice is enormous.

He left the table and came towards me.

"Won't you sit down?" he said.

"Thank you," I said, and took the chair he had pointed at.

"Do you smoke?" he asked.

"Yes, thank you," I said.

After he had lit our cigarettes, he remained standing. "And what can I do for you?" he asked.

I said, "My husband told me I was mad and that I should go and have my head seen to."

He gave a contemptuous laugh.

"I shouldn't take any notice of this if I were you," he said; "husbands always say this sort of thing, you know."

"But this isn't why I came here," I said, raising my eyes and looking at him as he was sitting down on the long, hard couch, of the same old-fashioned kind I had seen in Gordon's consulting room in Welbeck Street on that one occasion when I had gone there; it was covered in cinnamon-brown corded cloth and there was a small hole from a cigarette burn on the rolled-over head-end. He can't be that fussy if he doesn't get it mended, I thought.

"I wanted to ask you why Gordon died."

"Oh, Gordon," he said, rising; "Gordon."

He stood straight, tilting his head back, his hands in his pockets.

"I did not know about his death at the time it happened," I said; "I might have never known at all. I heard about it much later—by a queer chance. And after this, for some weeks, I kept seeing Gordon in the streets, walking towards me, coming nearer. But it was not Gordon, it was some complete stranger who did not even look like him, and I had to tell myself, Don't be ridiculous, it isn't Gordon, it can't be Gordon, because Gordon is dead."

"You think this is strange?" he asked.

"Yes," I said, "don't you?"

"No," he said.

"Perhaps it was a kind of punishment," I said, "because I did not feel anything at the time when I heard about it. I was quite heartless, I can't understand it. But then, of course, I was not prepared for it."

It had been a mild, sunny day in September, in the early afternoon. I entered the house in Campden Hill and walked carefully up the stairs so as not to dislodge the sheets of newspaper laid over the treads; they were carpeted in Venetian red to match the new brocaded wallpaper. I did not like the colour. It had been chosen by the American with whom I was living.

On the landing I was met by one of the workmen who were decorating the first floor.

"There's been a call for you, madam, while you were out," he said; "you're to ring them back," and preceding me into the front room, he shouted to his mate: "Where you put it? You took it down, didn't you?"

The mate, standing on a stepladder, swivelled on his heels and raised his eyes to the ceiling. "It's in that corner over there," he said, and he read the number out to me. It was a number with a Welbeck exchange. I laughed at their way of taking down messages and went to the adjoining room where the telephone was placed on a kitchen chair.

My call was answered by a man with a cheerful voice which I placed as minor public school, Uppingham, Radley, or Lancing perhaps.

I told him my name and why I was calling.

"What a charming name you've got," he said, "Louisa. Most intriguing."

"But it doesn't mean anything to you, does it?" I asked.

"I wish it did," he said.

"This must be a mistake, then," I remarked, and was on the point of ringing off when he said, clearly having time on his hands and intending to while it away, "Hold on, wait a minute. I might be able to help you, after all. Now, this house here is full with nothing but psychiatrists."

My heart gave a leap, as it always did at the mention of this profession. "Oh, yes," I said, hoping he would not notice the trembling of my voice.

"Maybe one of my *confrères* wanted to speak to you," he said. "Just think. Who are the psychiatrists you happen to know?"

"I only know one," I said, struggling for breath.

"What's his name?" he asked.

"Gordon," I said. "Richard Gordon."

There was a pause.

Then he said, "Well, I suppose that settles it. He certainly did not ring you."

"How do you mean?" I asked. I was furious. I thought: I know he's got married. What had that to do with me? That was after he threw me out. And trust Leonie Beck to make it her business to have let me know. She would.

He said, "He's dead, of course."

"No," I said. "It's not—are you sure?" My heart was calm and steady. I was empty of all feeling.

"But you must have known," he said; "it was in all the papers."

"I never read the papers," I said. "But are you sure?"

"Quite sure," he said.

"But he was too young to die," I said; "he was only—now—forty-nine."

"Correct," he said.

"What did he die of?" I asked. "As far as I know, there was nothing wrong with him."

"Oh, these things happen, you know," he said pleasantly. "But you intrigue me, you know. You have a fascinating voice. I wish I could meet you."

I laughed. "I'll come to you one day when I want my head seen to," I said, and put the receiver down.

I rang up Leonie Beck.

"I've just heard Gordon is dead," I said.

"Oh, yes, poor Richard," she cooed tearfully; "didn't you know?"

"I didn't," I said.

"But you must have read it in the papers," she said.

"I didn't see it," I said. "How did he die?"

"It was a double suicide, you might say," she said, "because he took poison and cut his veins in the bath. The actual cause of death was drowning in the bath."

"When was this?" I asked.

"Oh, quite a time ago," she said; "let me see. It's September now. It was around Christmas. Before or after Christmas. I can't remember exactly."

"It must have been after," I said, "because I rang him up and wanted to see him. I wanted him to give me some advice about a man, an American—anyway, I spoke to him on the phone. And I do know it was the sixth of January, because that night I went to see my cousin because it was her birthday."

"Yes, you are right," she said, "and it must have been just a day or so after this. Because we all of us had barely got back into our jogtrot after the holidays and New Year."

"Why did he do it?" I asked.

"I don't know," she said; "but his old teacher—his analyst he'd gone back to—she had died, she was very old, about eighty. But that was some time before. I'm convinced that if she had been alive she would have held him and carried him through."

"So you've no idea why he did it?" I asked.

"No," she said, and added tearfully, "poor Richard."

"Yes," I said.

"One thing is certain, though," she said with a firmer voice. "He certainly did not premeditate it. He can't have planned it a long time in advance. Because he did it after lunch. And he had two patients put down in his book for the afternoon. He was a most conscientious person. He would have cancelled his sessions if he'd thought of it ahead."

"I see," I said.

"Such a brilliant man," she said, resuming her tearful voice, "and doing so well, just getting up a really good practice. And married for only two months. So dreadful for the wife. Probably—I should say—something to do with his potency troubles. Of course, I always used to feel so sorry for you while you were his girl-friend. You must have been so sad."

"I was never sad with him," I said. "I don't know what gave you this idea."

"Oh, but you must have been," she said, her voice full of motherly concern, "being the girl-friend of an impotent man is always miserable. But he was so amusing, of course. Such good company." She paused. I heard her sigh. She added: "And you yourself were not always quite—not that I blame you, it's so understandable, of course—but if you had not taunted him over his failing, which he couldn't help, unfortunately, he would not have behaved the way he did to you. You were in a dreadful state that night when you came to my flat. Any man can get violent if you make fun of him for being impotent. No wonder he attacked you and mauled you."

"Look here," I said, "now that he's dead, I'd better tell you once and for all. He was the most virile man I've ever known."

"Are you sure?" she asked in a pained voice. "I'd no idea," she added petulantly.

"Quite sure," I said; "he always went on and on interminably and I thought he'd never end. Sometimes it was more than I could take."

"But that's not nice either," she said in an offended tone of voice; "that must have been rather horrible for you."

"I put up with it," I said.

"Well," she said, still offended, "you amaze me." And when I kept silent, she asked, "Have you been anywhere nice this summer?"

I never found out who had rung me up on that afternoon.

Now Crombie looked at me keenly. "How did you come to know Richard?" he asked. "Funny, you know, I haven't thought of him for years."

"I can't understand this," I said. "How couldn't you? When I think—"

"Ah, yes," he said, "I can quite see it. Richard was very fascinating to women. Very fascinating," and he retreated to the corner behind the couch and leaned against the wall, his hands still in his pockets.

"How did you meet him?" he repeated.

I said, "He picked me up, in a way I'd never been picked up before, and he got hold of me in a way that had never happened to me before, and he treated me in a way nobody ever treated me, before or after,"

"Did you know his wife?" he asked.

"No," I said.

He came out of his corner and stopped in front of the couch, looking at the window before him. I noticed that it was un-curtained and that the panes were whitewashed. One could do anything here and nobody would know. Neither see nor hear, because it was tucked away at the very end of the passage.

He said, narrowing his eyes and pushing his lips forwards, "She was—quite a nice little thing—I suppose."

I thought: That's good enough for me. He's made it quite plain.

He moved away and perched on the rolled-over top of the couch. "You know," he said, "with men like Richard, there's always just one very valuable woman in their lives. Only one." And he looked at me longingly.

He rose and went back into the corner, leaning against it. "Now, tell me how you met him," he said.

"It was nine years ago, in June," I said, and I told him about

Shepherds, about Gordon's finger pressing on my pulse, and about how I had to go with him. I skipped all our talk, mentioned the club in Brook Street, got straight into the tired dusty garden with the stone bench, and concluded by saying, "I was terribly ashamed and annoyed with myself," thinking recklessly, What does it matter? I didn't come here to make a good impression on him.

"How long were you with him?" he asked.

"Less than a year," I said.

"Well," said Crombie, "what do you want me to do?" He detached himself from his corner and came over to where I was sitting. "Look here, my sweet," he said, "the man is dead. I can't give him back to you."

"Yes," I said.

"In a way it's an advantage that he's dead," he remarked. "It makes it better, don't you think?"

"Yes, it does," I said. "A Sicilian once said to me, 'When you love a woman, it is best to kill her. Then you know where she is and what she is doing.' "

Crombie laughed.

"Isn't that how you mean it?" I asked. "He is dead now. And I know where he is and what he's doing. But I never wanted him to die."

"Didn't you?" he asked, smiling indulgently.

"No," I said, "and he killed himself. Very efficiently and thoroughly. Without my help."

"Well," said Crombie, "if you say so, I must believe you. You are quite sincere in what you believe, no doubt."

I got annoyed. It sounded as though he, very tactfully, was telling me he knew I was lying.

"But I didn't want him to die," I said, "and you know yourself how he died. I never came near him at the time. He'd thrown me out—ages ago, before. Besides, I never liked him. I didn't like his body. I always made difficulties."

"Did you really?" asked Crombie. "Then, you didn't like him as a lover?"

"Yes, I did," I said. "I made difficulties, but once he started, I was dying for it. But I wasn't fond of him. Because he was beastly. And he never touched me at all."

"How's that?" asked Crombie.

"He never kissed me once," I said.

"Because you didn't want it?" asked Crombie.

"Don't be ridiculous," I said; "of course I wanted it. But he never did."

"You minded that? Did you?" he asked.

"Yes, very much," I said.

"You minded it but you put up with it, is that it?" he asked.

"Yes," I said.

"Of course," he remarked, "I can quite see how exasperating Richard must have been. You must have been quite pleased when he died."

"Yes, I was," I said. I lowered my head and covered my eyes with my hands. "I was ashamed of being so pleased, but it's true."

"Well, that's quite natural," he remarked. "He must have been very awkward in his behaviour to you. Plunging straight in, without any caresses. Somewhat insulting."

"He always did," I said. "Sometimes he couldn't even wait till I got my clothes off. I'd come in through the door and he'd put me on the floor as I was."

"Now, that's rather charming, though, I must say," remarked Crombie, tilting his head back and smiling. "You know, he celebrated his marriage by whoring all over the place."

"How extraordinary," I said, "With me—he didn't. He

couldn't. At least, that's what he told me. And I think everything he told me was true."

Crombie said, "Obviously what he told you, in your case, was true. He had a different kind of attachment to you. In the case of his marriage he wanted to shoot his bolt. He wasn't very keen to get married, you know."

I said, "I always knew his second marriage didn't mean a thing to him. But still—all the more so—I mean, one doesn't go and kill oneself because of it."

"Tell me, my sweet," he said, "you are married yourself, aren't you? To the man who says you're mad?"

I laughed. "Yes, I am," I said, "but Gordon was before my husband. Ages before. My husband's got nothing to do with it. I only wanted to know why Gordon killed himself."

"I am not a marriage counsellor, you know," said Crombie. "When people come to me and say, will you put my marriage right? I turn them away. I don't know myself what will come out once they start."

"You are being idiotic," I said heatedly. I was not on my best manners any more. I was not even on my ordinary manners—in fact, I had not talked this way to anyone since Gordon. "You are barking up the wrong tree," I said. "I am happily married. And my husband and I never quarrel."

"I see," said Crombie. "Now, tell me, what am I going to do with you?"

"I don't know," I said.

"Will you come again?" he asked.

"If you'll have me," I said, flooded by relief.

"When can you come? Wednesday? Suit you?" he asked.

"Whenever you say," I said.

"Twelve o'clock?" he asked, walking to a desk with a pulled-out flap and leafing through a book.

"Yes," I said, rising; "good-bye. And thank you."

"Good-bye," he said, and he remained at his desk, not looking at me, while I hurriedly gathered up my fur and, clutching it in both my arms, too hasty to carry it more becomingly, left the room.

The passage did not seem so exceedingly long to me this time, and upon getting out into the street I thought, He didn't even ask for my address. If I never went to see him again, he wouldn't even know where to send his bill to. Most unbusiness-like. And he called me 'my sweet.' Twice. Frightfully unbusiness-like, too.

I stopped and put on my mink coat. I was feeling marvellously at peace.

Chapter

Twenty-one

The second time I went to see Crombie, he asked me to tell him about my life, from childhood onwards, saying, "We'd better get down to some work now."

I did not know what he meant. All I wanted was to talk about Gordon. But I did what he asked.

The next time I went to see him, Crombie told me I should lie down on the couch and just say anything that came into my head.

I was astonished. I told him it was exactly what Gordon had made me do sometimes, when pulling me up by my hair out of my sleep in the middle of the night, and he laughed about it. He laughed again when I told him how Gordon used to slap me and twist my wrist when I had not wanted to answer his questions.

"It's quite easy," he said; "there's nothing to be afraid of. Just lie down."

I felt awkward and constrained about it, nevertheless, but when he asked me if I wanted a cigarette and an ashtray, I felt more at ease; I thanked him and said I would not smoke.

I stretched out more comfortably. I could not see him. He was sitting at the small round table behind me, and I could hear him strike a match.

"Start with what is in your mind just now," he said.

I felt ashamed. Then I remembered Gordon's "Whatever you say, it's nothing to what my patients tell me," and I entwined my fingers closely and said, "I've just been wondering if I won't get disarranged, lying down like this and then getting up again, because I've got the curse today. You know, it doesn't mean a thing to me now, any more, and yet in the old days I was besides myself with worry if I was a day late. It was like the joke about the girl going to the chemist's and saying, 'Please give me a packet of sanitary towels, thank God.' But now—I just know it's got to come. Because my husband—when I sleep with him—what there is of it—he can't do it properly. For the last two years it's been like this—I loathe it. It's a travesty of—it's revolting."

"Ah, yes," said Crombie. He sounded cheerful.

"I suppose I shouldn't have married him," I said, "but what was I to do? And Gordon was dead, anyway."

"Then, if you were happy in bed," said Crombie, "you think you would be completely happy? Because you told me you were happily married."

"Yes," I said, "but that's not possible. Even if my husband . . . Because I was only happy in bed with Gordon."

For the rest of the time I talked about nothing but Gordon; about his jokes, about the "cemetery," how he had used me like a boy, how he had beaten me up, how he had thrown me out . . .

"And what I minded most about it," I said, "was the way he had to fling this father-figure business at me. And it was nonsense, too. I never thought about my father till I met Gordon and he started in on him. He really invented him."

Crombie laughed.

I never mentioned my father again, nor did he.

It was only the third time I went to see him that Crombie asked me for my address, and when he was astonished that I was staying at a hotel, I explained to him that my husband was an antiquarian, a continental link-up with Sotheby's, that we were living abroad, and that I would be staying only for six weeks. I was afraid that he, upon hearing this, would put down his notebook and tell me it was not worth his while to continue. But he made no comment.

He made no comment either when I said that I had been waiting to see him for the last eight years, ever since Gordon's death, and how I had kept putting it off, for fear he would ridicule my preoccupation, saying something like, "If that's all you've got to worry about. . . ."

After the first time lying down on the couch, I lost any feeling of constraint. And as I kept talking, most of the time, about Gordon, I thought he would get sick and tired of hearing about him, but he often laughed and was obviously amused, and this reassured me.

"Why don't you leave your husband?" asked Crombie one day, suddenly, after I had told him about the Belgrave Park Hotel, and how much trouble Gordon had taken over me, even going there to see it for himself, to find out whether it tallied with my description.

"It would be wrong of me," I said. "After all, we've been married for four years now, and he likes being married to me; I never bore him. Most women do, though. And he is what is called a model husband."

"Is that all?" asked Crombie. "Then all you feel for him is a sense of duty."

"Yes, that's true," I said.

"What would your mother say about your situation now, if she were alive?" asked Crombie.

"She'd say, 'Be unfaithful, if you like, but be careful he won't find out.' " I added, "She'd be indulgent."

"And what would your grandmother say?" he asked.

"She'd tell me to be faithful," I said. "She'd say, 'He's decent and considerate to you, he doesn't drink, he doesn't gamble, you've even got a mink coat, and you could have an ermine coat, too, so what more do you want?' "

"I see," said Crombie.

"My grandmother was full of a sense of duty. She loathed my grandfather, but she never looked at another man. But I haven't got her strength. I don't want to carry on, and I don't want to break. I don't know what to do. You know, Goethe said the best thing about Hamlet anybody ever said. He said that Hamlet was a man who had not the strength to carry his burden and who neither had the strength to roll it off his shoulders. That's how I feel. But my grandmother was strong. She could carry her burden."

"Then, you really would leave your husband if you could?" asked Crombie.

"Yes," I said, "it's true. But I'm shattered. I've never known it. It's never occurred to me before, the idea of walking out on him. Not till this moment. Do you know, when I left home now and came to London, I only came to see you because of Gordon, and now it's turned out that my marriage doesn't mean a thing to me and it's all dust and ashes."

"Just go on talking," said Crombie.

When I left him that day, he said to me, "Gordon is dead and you are alive, and I want to keep you alive, husband or no husband."

On the following day when I lay down on the couch, I said, "I had lunch yesterday with an old acquaintance. He was James's partner in the art gallery—I met my husband through him, you know, by the way—and he told me that James is dead. That's the rich man I told you about, who kept me for two years. He died only three weeks ago. Of a bad heart. So you see, he never committed suicide because of me, though he said he would, when I left him."

"Would you have liked him to?" asked Crombie.

"No," I said, "certainly not. It would not even have flattered me. I just didn't care enough for him, either way."

"For how many men did you really care?" asked Crombie.

"Only for Gordon," I said.

"And do you think Gordon loved you?" asked Crombie.

"Yes," I said; "he never kissed me and he never cuddled me, and he loved me desperately. And it didn't get lukewarm as time went on. It got worse and worse. He bit into me more and more savagely."

Crombie said, "With Gordon you came, as near as you could, to the perfect union. Has it never occurred to you that there is a connection between love and death? Without Gordon's savagery, there would have been no love."

"Yes," I said, "I know. And that's one of the things my husband minds about me. He says love should be humourous and light and full of fun, and to me the idea that love should go with chuckles is simply ghastly. It turns my stomach. And he tells me I have no sense of humour. And you know, his humour—it's revolting—it's shocking—" And I tossed on the couch and twisted my fingers.

Crombie was silent.

I said, "But it's really revolting. You know what he says, when he wants to? He says he wants to blow his nose and get rid of his slime. And that's supposed to be a joke. He thinks it's funny. I've never told him, though, what I feel. What's the use?"

"Ah, yes," said Crombie, "and I quite agree with you. It is revolting."

I said, "You know, my husband and I, when we were in London last year in November, we went back to Spain by car, and on the way we went to see the *châteaux de la Loire*. He knew them well but I'd never been, and he only made the detour for my sake, so I should see them. And in one of them, in Villandry, I think, we were taken to the gardens, and the guide said he'd show us the one part which was called 'the garden of love,' and when we got there, I saw nothing but patterns made up of cut box, well trimmed, of course, and I couldn't see what it had to do with love. But when the guide explained it, it became perfectly clear. And so true. The pattern in the first square was hearts and flowers. That was happy love. The second was fans and butterflies. That was gay love. The third square was knives and daggers. That was tragic love. And the fourth square was broken hearts and shattered flowers. That was mad love. And then I thought, no wonder my husband and I are the way we are; we can never get together, because we are in different squares. Gordon and I—we were in the same square—we were knives and daggers."

"Ah, yes," said Crombie; "this is just what I meant, with love and death. But what do you think would have happened if Gordon had not thrown you out? Do you think you would have been able to reform him?"

"Of course not," I said, "we would have gone on and on, from bad to worse."

"And what would have happened in the end, do you think?" he asked.

"He would have killed me," I said, "or I would have killed him."

"You wanted to kill him?" asked Crombie.

"No," I said, "I didn't—all right— Yes. I did want to."

"Do you know what was between you and Gordon?" said Crombie. "It was not love and hate. It was love and destruction. I knew it the first time you came to see me."

I did not speak.

"And I can also tell you now why he threw you out," said Crombie. He paused. I heard him strike a match. He continued, "Because Gordon developed too many kinks with you, and he exploited you. He knew what he meant with his 'I know when I'm well off,' and you let yourself be exploited. What other woman would have stood him, the way he was with you? One night, and out. But not you. That's when he got scared; I can see it quite clearly now. That's why he went back into analysis and got rid of you. You thought you displeased him. You pleased him only too well. He told you in so many words, too, but you did not understand him."

"Yes," I said; " 'I don't want to get rid of you but I've got to.' And he had a splitting headache. I still see him sitting there and lacing his shoe."

"And then he got married," said Crombie; "it was his last fling. His last attempt to straighten out. But he couldn't any more. The damage you'd done was too deep. He committed suicide soon after you went to see him, while you were living with that rich man, that one time, didn't he?"

"Yes," I said, "it must have been the day after."

"And when you heard about it, you were pleased," said Crombie.

"But I didn't kill him," I exclaimed, "I really didn't. He did it himself."

"But you wanted to, just the same," he said; "and you felt guilty about it, too, because his likeness kept haunting you in the streets, as you told me—every stranger was Gordon's ghost. You knew quite well you had had your share in killing him."

"Yes," I said, "I knew that somehow—only I didn't understand how—"

"And now you are still seeking for the perfect union," said

Crombie, "but he is holding you back. All the time. Do you believe in perfect love?"

"Not in marriage," I said; "marriage is all wrong. I didn't want to marry Gordon, either, I told you. I was glad when he said he wouldn't marry me."

"But outside of marriage," said Crombie, "do you believe it is possible?"

"Yes," I said, "but it's very rare."

"It is very rare," said Crombie; "but do you believe it?"

"Yes," I said, "I do," and I shifted myself on the couch and put my head lower down on the hard, flat cushion. I felt light and empty, absolved of responsibility and indecision.

Crombie said, "You must stop Gordon now from holding you back."

"Yes," I said, "I want to get rid of him."

"No, that would be too much," said Crombie. "We'll put him away, like a monument, shall we? With a wreath of flowers."

"Yes," I said.

Chapter

Twenty-two

It was my last week in London. It meant that I would be having only three more times with Crombie, and when I came to see him that Monday and reminded him of it, he said, "Ah, yes. Our time is running out. Lie down now."

I felt hurt that he had not said, at least, "What a pity," and because of this I said what I had intended not to say: "You know, when you rang me up this morning, in the hotel?"

"Yes," he said.

"And you asked if I could come this afternoon instead of at mid-day? And when I said it was all right, you said, 'I'm very much obliged to you.' And it made me furious."

"Why?" he asked.

"Because here I am," I said, "and I tell you things I've never told anyone else before, and then you say, 'I'm very much obliged to you.' Like a tradesman. Or like a tailor who's put off the hour of the fitting."

He laughed.

"What should I have said?" he asked.

"You should have said something less ghastly, just thank you, I suppose," I remarked; "and *à propos* of the tailor, my mother used to say there are four professions where the men are not men, I mean, one does not think of them as men—the hairdresser, the tailor, the room-service waiter, and the doctor. Because they all see women more or less in undress, and it doesn't count."

I paused. I thought he would laugh again. But he remained silent.

Then I went on to talk about my grandmother and my mother, and the rows they had over the servants, and how my mother liked to interfere and would find greasy unwashed saucepans in the kitchen cupboards and got the cook angry, till she upped and left, and how my grandmother had tried to stop her from stirring up trouble and had preferred to tolerate things rather than have the maids leaving.

Crombie said, "You are really talking about your own problem, aren't you? You are giving me various philosophies. Should one avoid a final break and put up with things as they are and carry on, or should one throw down the sponge and start with a clean slate? What would you like to do, if you could?"

"I'd like to live on my own again," I said.

"And what about love?" he asked.

I got cross. "That must come of its own," I said; "one cannot chase it." And as he did not speak, I added, *"L'amour ne se commande pas."*

"Do you want it?" he asked.

"Yes, of course I do," I said.

"Or do you want to go back and keep yourself frustrated again?" he asked.

"No," I said.

He said, "You are very much alive now, and I don't want you to die. I don't mean die literally, of course. I don't want you to sit and sort out your memories and say, 'I've had this and I want no more.' You do want more, do you?"

"Yes, I do," I said.

"That's all I wanted to hear," he remarked.

When I went to see Crombie next, which was the last but one time, I asked him to have the bill ready.

"I don't really know what to charge you," he said.

"Charge me up to the hilt," I said, flaring up; "don't be so idiotic. I wouldn't have come to you if I couldn't have afforded you."

"So be it," he said. "Go and lie down now."

On the last day, he received me much as usual and told me to lie down.

"It's a fine day today," I said, "very mild for this time of the year, and I've put on a white woollen dress. It's extravagant to wear white in winter. White is the colour of impotence, because when you can't write, the paper stays white and empty. That's not from me, of course, that's from Mallarmé. Mallarmé, too, had a thing about women's long hair. He loved it. I've got long hair, but it's no use to me. For my mother it was all right, though. When my mother was a little girl, she could wear her long hair open down her back, on one day of the year, for the emperor's birthday. Franz-Josef was very old, he reigned for sixty-two years, but now he's dead. For me it's too late."

"Go on," said Crombie.

"I can't," I said. "My mind is a complete blank. Like the white paper. I'm powerless."

"Let your mind roam," he said.

"I had a farewell dinner party yesterday," I said, "with my cousin Sylvia," and I proceeded with a funny story she had told me: One of our uncles once woke in the middle of the night after having composed a poem in his dream. He got up and hastened to write it down, telling himself while doing so, "I'm really marvellously gifted." Then he went back to sleep. In the morning he looked at the poem. It was a fairly well-known poem by Goethe.

"What was it about?" asked Crombie.

I said, "The gist is, if you keep yourself from doing what you want to do, you'll wander like a tired guest on this dim earth."

"Go on," he said.

"There's another much more peculiar poem by Goethe," I said; "it's never in the collected official works. It's about himself, how he gets roused to desire at the most unsuitable moments, for instance, when he stands in church in front of the crucified Christ-figure. And when he is in bed with the pretty young servant girl, he cannot make love to her, and is quite perplexed about it. He gets out of bed, his desire returns, but he spends the rest of the night sitting up and thinking. It ends by saying, two levers are at work to keep the earthly merry-go-round spinning—one is duty, but stronger still is love."

Crombie said, "Ah, yes."

Then, like a chamois leaping from crag to crag, I abruptly landed on another peak, on the *Marienbader Elegie*, which Goethe had written at the age of seventy-five after having been turned down by the nineteen-year-old Ulrike. "She was a chill, dim, anaemic goat," I said. "Imagine refusing Goethe. Can you imagine any woman refusing Goethe?"

"Yes, I can," said Crombie.

I went on about Goethe, till I heard him getting up from his chair and knew it was time to go.

"Have you got the bill for me?" I asked.

"Here it is," he said, walking with me to the desk and picking up an envelope from the pulled-out flap.

"I'll pay you straightaway," I said, tearing open the envelope more violently than I had intended to. My hand was shaking. "One hundred pounds," I said, getting out my cheque book. "I wish you'd charged me more."

"Why?" he asked.

"Because you've sorted me out," I said, "though differently from the way I thought you would."

"Ah, yes," he said.

He watched me as I wrote rather fast, in order to steady my hand, filled in the stub, tore the cheque off the book, and placed it on the desk.

I picked up my bag and straightened up.

He took my hand.

"You've been a real joy to me," he remarked.

I tried to force a smile.

"Come back to me," he said, "if anything major happens. No, come back to me anyway, whenever you feel like it."

"You are very kind," I said with a faint voice.

He released my hand. He moved away from me and said, still with his back turned, and with his eyes on the floor: "Not at all kind. It's only natural."

I did not speak.

He turned round after a while and walked to the window and said, keeping his glance on the whitewashed panes, "What are you going to do now?"

"I don't know," I said, "I'm—I'm terribly unsettled."

He remarked, still gazing at the window, "You must follow your heart and damn the consequences."

"It's not possible," I said.

"Yes, it is," he said.

He turned and faced me. He watched me as I put my handbag on the desk. He remained silent.

I went up to him slowly and folded my arms round his neck and laid my head on his broad powerful chest. He clasped me firmly and I lay against him, trembling.

"My sweetheart," he said, and I calmed down. "Put your lips

up to me," he said. I tilted my face up to his and he kissed me long and slowly, then crushed me to his body suddenly, held me for an instant and released me.

"That was very sweet of you," he said, "my sweet Louisa."

"Will you really have me?" I asked.

"Yes," he said, "for as long as you want. If you want, for ever."

I rested my head against him and closed my eyes.

"Do you know how old I am?" he asked.

"No," I said.

"Shall I tell you?" he asked.

"No, I don't want to know," I said.

"I don't deserve you," he said, "I am very old. As old as the emperor. Will you open your hair for me?"

"Yes," I said.

"Are you sure you don't mind?" he asked.

"No," I said; "I don't care about anything, because I love you."

"I used to see your knees when you moved on the couch," he said; "that was something, but it was not enough. Come and lie down with me now."

It was I did not know how much later when he said, "At last I've made you cry out. I should have done this much sooner, the first time you came in. You have that magic in you. Open your eyes now and look at me."

I moved my head and kept my eyes closed. He was still lying half across me, crushing the metal loop of one of my suspenders into my thigh, with one hand slipped underneath my petticoat, covering my breast.

I was afraid to lose the last aftermath of the bliss which had streamed through me till I had wanted to melt away.

"Open your eyes. Only for one moment," he said; "then you can close them again."

And I obeyed.

About the Author

Edith Templeton was born in Prague in 1916 and spent much of her childhood in a castle in the Bohemian countryside. She was educated at a French lycée in Prague and left that city in 1938 to marry an Englishman. During her years in Britain she worked in the Office of the Chief Surgeon for the U.S. Army in Cheltenham, and then became a captain in the British Army, working as a high-level conference interpreter. Her short stories began to appear in the *New Yorker* in the fifties, and over the next several decades she published a number of novels, as well as a popular travel book, *The Surprise of Cremona*, in the United Kingdom. Her most recent book is *The Darts of Cupid and Other Stories* (2002).

Mrs. Templeton left England in 1956 to live in India with her second husband, a celebrated cardiologist. She has since lived in various parts of Europe and now makes her home in Bordighera, on Italy's Ligurian coast.

A Note on the Type

Pierre Simon Fournier *le jeune,* who designed the type used in this book, was both an originator and a collector of types. His services to the art of printing were his design of letters, his creation of ornaments and initials, and his standardization of type sizes. His types are old style in character and sharply cut. In 1764 and 1766 he published his *Manuel Typographique,* a treatise on the history of French types and printing, on typefounding in all its details, and on what many consider his most important contribution to typography—the measurement of type by the point system.

Composed by Creative Graphics,
Allentown, Pennsylvania

Printed and bound by R.R. Donnelley & Sons,
Harrisonburg, Virginia

Book design by M. Kristen Bearse